"It really is   **."**

Wayne worked
hardened every ~~~~~~ ~~~~~~ ~~ight of a world without
his father. "If we can pull this off and bring my dad
comfort in the last weeks of his life, it could be
worth it."

"When you put it that way..." Paisley wiped her tears
with the backs of her hands. "Maybe we should
throw caution to the wind and go for it?"

"You think?" Relief and the thought of doing
something—anything—proactive toward helping his
dad made his pulse race.

"For the record, you have to know this could end in
disaster."

"True."

"Just give me a couple days to wrap my head
around the logistics."

"Deal." He stood, then crossed the short distance
between them to shake her hand. When their
hands touched, was it his imagination, or was there
a spark that had never been there before?

Not cool. Sparks were the last thing he needed.

Dear Reader,

At the time I'm writing this, the US has just witnessed the heartbreaking devastation of hurricanes Harvey and Irma. What an awful pair, right? In Oklahoma, we've had a lovely start to our autumn. Warm, sunny days and cool nights—pleasant enough to make it inconceivable how much damage is taking place in other parts of the country.

My thoughts and prayers go out to all who were affected by these terrible storms. Hope your lives soon get back to normal. In a few weeks, I'm traveling to Florida for a long-planned conference and I dread seeing homes and businesses that didn't fare so well.

In Wayne and Paisley's story, they're both dealing with the kind of pain that can't be fixed with a hammer and nails or fresh coat of paint. Wayne has learned his father is dying of cancer, and oddly enough, his best friend and very pregnant neighbor, Paisley, is the only one who can help. To find out how, you'll have to dive into their story.

Happy reading!

Laura Marie

COWBOY SEAL DADDY

—

LAURA MARIE ALTOM

⬥ HARLEQUIN® WESTERN ROMANCE

Recycling programs
for this product may
not exist in your area.

ISBN-13: 978-1-335-69963-3

Cowboy SEAL Daddy

Copyright © 2018 by Laura Marie Altom

Printed in U.S.A.

www.Harlequin.com

Laura Marie Altom is a bestselling and award-winning author who has penned nearly fifty books. After college (go, Hogs!), Laura Marie did a brief stint as an interior designer before becoming a stay-at-home mom to boy-girl twins and a bonus son. Always an avid romance reader, she knew it was time to try her hand at writing when she found herself replotting the afternoon soaps.

When not immersed in her next story, Laura plays video games, tackles Mount Laundry and, of course, reads romance!

Laura loves hearing from readers at either PO Box 2074, Tulsa, OK 74101, or by email, balipalm@aol.com.

Love winning fun stuff? Check out lauramariealtom.com.

Books by Laura Marie Altom

Harlequin Western Romance

Cowboy SEALs

Visit the Author Profile page
at Harlequin.com for more titles.

For my mom, Louise. I love you. xoxo

Chapter One

"*This team sucks!* You look more like rubber ducks than SEALs. If it was up to me, I'd strip your Tridents and replace them with flight attendant wings!"

Navy SEAL Wayne Brustanovitch sat alongside the rest of his twelve-man team on the *Mark V Special Operations Craft* jetting past the Coronado coast at forty-five knots while their pissed-off CO handed them their asses on a platter. It was 0300, and they'd been running beach landing drills for the past eight hours.

It was late March. Cold, wet, tired and hungry, Wayne needed a beer, burger and bed. Hell—at this point, he wasn't even choosy about the order.

Twelve hours later, they'd finally achieved an insertion time their CO deemed acceptable—at least good enough to earn a meal and hot shower.

"How's your dad doing?" Logan Crenshaw served as the closest thing Wayne had to a brother. While they dressed before heading for the chow hall, Wayne welcomed the chance to run a predicament by his roommate and friend.

"Bad. Our last call, he said the doctor had basically given him a death sentence."

"Damn…" Logan whistled. "That's rough. Sorry, man."

"Thanks. But that's not the half of it." He pulled on boxers, then gray sweats. "He told me that it's his dying wish to see me married and to hold his grandchild in his arms."

"Ouch. Way to pour on the parental guilt."

"No kidding, right?" Wayne added deodorant, then a white T-shirt with Navy written on the front.

"Too bad you can't rent a wife and kid, huh?"

"I wish. That's the only way I'd take vows again."

"Got nothing but love for you, brother. That sorry SOB can rot in hell."

A fist bump relayed Wayne's similar sentiment.

But the SEAL brother who'd broken ranks to cheat with Wayne's ex wasn't solely to blame. Like the old saying goes, "It takes two to tango," and Chelsea had lied and schemed right up to their marriage's official end.

Dressed, the two men joined the rest of their exhausted team in line for mystery meat and mashed potatoes. It wouldn't have mattered what was served. Wayne was hungry enough to eat cardboard—a good thing, considering the potatoes' dried consistency.

After another verbal lashing during their meal, the CO declared them officially dismissed until 0200 the next morning.

Since Logan was in an on-off relationship with a

Hooters waitress who had apparently decided to be back *on*, they'd driven separately to base.

Most of the single guys drove Mustangs or Chargers, but Wayne stayed true to his country roots by maintaining his red 1976 Ford F-150 Ranger truck. Of course, he'd souped up the engine and cab, but the original body was pristine.

He might be a SEAL, but he was also a cowboy through and through. Next to him on the custom red leather seat was his trusty straw cowboy hat. The thing looked like it had been trampled by a herd of mustangs, but he never felt truly dressed without it. As soon as he put in his twenty years until retirement, he'd move back to the family ranch. Wayne knew his dad wanted him there now, but with eighteen months remaining on his current enlistment, even if he opted for early retirement, he couldn't just tell his CO he was leaving.

Traffic was hell on I-5 and it took forty minutes to reach his apartment complex.

As he pulled into the lot, his neighbor Paisley Carter struggled to roll out of her friend Monica's low-slung Jaguar convertible. The two of them owned an interior design business located in a trendy part of town. Monica, who was hot as hell, once had a thing with Logan, which made her off-limits to anyone else on their team. Whereas Monica was pure sex in her tight black dress and the red-soled shoes every woman on the planet seemed to go nuts for, Paisley was more the take-home-to-Mom type in weird pink pants and a white blouse big enough to be a painter's smock.

She was adorable—even more so pregnant.

She was also a good girl who'd fallen prey to a two-timing bastard. The guy who'd knocked her up didn't seem to be in the picture, which made Wayne want to punch him into the next county for leaving Paisley in such a rough spot—especially with her crap car apparently in the shop again.

He knew firsthand how much it sucked being cheated on. A nice girl like Paisley didn't deserve that fate.

Like you did?

Squashing that old insecurity like the scorpion he'd found in his boot on their last Middle East mission, Wayne eliminated that line of thought.

After pulling into the first spot he saw, he killed the engine, then hopped out to help Paisley to her feet.

"Give me your hand," he said, looking past her to wave to Monica. "Hey. How's it going?"

"Great. How's Logan?"

"Good."

"I hate to hear that. In fact, I hate—"

"Excuse me," Paisley said. "Pregnant lady struggling to get out of this motorized skateboard."

"Sorry." Wayne skipped taking Paisley's hand in favor of scooping her into his arms. He knocked the Jag's door shut with his hip. "Catch you later, Monica."

"Bye. Tell Logan to suck it. Feel better, Paise!" The brunette gave them a backhanded wave before revving the engine and peeling out of the lot.

Wayne said, "Logan's an idiot for letting her go."

"You're an idiot for lusting after her. You do realize she's an heiress and more high maintenance than my car—that's broken down again."

Horsing around, Wayne feigned a dreamy sigh. "A man can fantasize about Monica. Not that heap of metal you call a car."

"Be nice." Paisley landed a light smack to the back of his head, then flung her arms around his neck while he took the stairs two at a time. "How's Logan doing with their breakup? Monica's a tad bitter."

"No kidding?" Wayne laughed. "I never would've guessed. So, what's wrong with your car this time?"

"Needs a new transmission."

"Ouch." He set her on her feet in front of her apartment door. They'd been neighbors for a few years. They barbecued a couple weekends each month and whenever he was deployed, she watched the cactus his mother had given him. She made cookies for him and Logan at Christmas and a special meal for them on Veteran's Day. She would make some lucky guy an incredible…

Wife.

Logan's locker room joke might not be such a bad idea. Obviously, Wayne would never be in the market to marry again for real. But he was totally on board with a rental spouse.

The trick would be convincing Paisley that taking his money for posing as his temporary wife would be a mutually beneficial arrangement as opposed to charity.

Over too many beers at the complex pool party last Fourth of July, she'd admitted Monica had bought her a car for her birthday, but she'd made her friend take it back. She hadn't gone into too much detail, but Wayne gathered the gist was that she'd been raised by a single mom who'd had no qualms about taking all the hand-outs she could get.

She opened her door and now eyed him funny. "Everything all right? You look almost as green as I usually do."

"Actually, I have something I'd like to run by you. Want to grab a bite to eat? Maybe Italian?"

She blanched.

"Your little one still making you sick?"

She nodded on her way into the living room. "He didn't get the memo that morning sickness isn't supposed to last day and night for months."

"Is there anything you do crave?" Wayne shut the door and followed her into her apartment.

"Gummy bears and beef jerky—oh, and split pea soup. But with my car out of commission, I haven't been to the store."

Now Wayne was the one making a face. "You do know that's a nasty food combo?"

She patted her baby bump. "Try explaining that to this guy. These days, he calls all the shots."

"Hang tight. I'll grab everything."

"Wayne, no. I'm not even hungry. Monica brought me home for a nap." She stretched out on the sofa with a soft sigh.

"Great. You have a snooze, and by the time I get back, you'll be ready for a talk."

"Why?" She rolled onto her side, jamming a hot pink pillow between her knees. What was it with her and loud colors?

"Does it matter?" He didn't blame her for being suspicious.

"I suppose not." She'd closed her eyes and, at least for a moment, looked at peace. Then she opened one eye, staring dead at him. "But it is curious. Why would a career military man and confirmed bachelor suddenly want to suck up to little ol' me?" Both eyes now open, she cocked her head, shooting him the cutest devilish grin. How had he never noticed her pistachio-colored gaze?

"You know," he said with a forced chuckle. "That is a good question. One I will be happy to answer once I have you all buttered up with gummy bears, beef jerky and split pea soup."

BEFORE PAISLEY RECEIVED an adequate answer from Wayne, he was gone. Just as well. Her baby was practicing soccer kicks against her ribs and the pain made a task as simple as talking too big of an effort to enjoy—even with a too-handsome-for-his-own-good SEAL like Wayne.

She'd crushed on him for three years.

Ever since watching him move into the apartment next-door, hauling boxes and furniture bare-chested past her living room window all day long. Sadly, she'd soon enough learned the score for not only him, but his SEAL friends. They were a cocky lot—admittedly for good reason—but the constant string of bikini models and flight attendants made it clear that a plain Jane such as herself was strictly friend material.

Probably a good thing.

If Paisley had managed to catch hard-bodied Wayne, she wouldn't know what to do with him. Guys like him no doubt possessed skills she'd never dreamed of in certain explicit areas…

Hands to superheated cheeks, she grinned.

Yes, it was a good thing Wayne had already left.

She was also thankful for the fact that she'd firmly sworn off all males over the age of three months. Dr. Dirtbag had burned her badly enough to leave scars.

Paisley had met him at the corner Starbucks.

David was cute in a glasses-wearing, nerdy way. As an ER doctor, he'd always been dressed in scrubs and brimming with thrilling stories of the latest lives he'd saved. It had never occurred to her that he could have been lying—stupid given her family history. But she supposed if you wanted to believe something badly enough, you did. She'd never thought to question why she only saw him early weekday mornings. He was a doctor. Of course, his schedule would be tricky. Any amount of time he'd carved for them had been precious. Their routine had been lovely. She'd prepare him breakfast, they'd make love, shower, then go about their days.

Never once had she thought to question why in over three months of dating, she'd never seen him at night. Or why his car was crappier than hers. Or why his scrubs were faded and frayed from too many washings.

Stupid, stupid, stupid.

Her pregnancy had been an accident.

When she told him he was going to be a father, she'd expected happy tears and an engagement ring. She'd daydreamed of finally living out her lifelong vision of belonging to a real family.

What had she gotten?

Ugly accusations.

You got pregnant on purpose, didn't you? Just like your mom did with all her men, you set out to trap me.

Nothing could have been further from the truth. Nothing could have cut deeper than to be compared to her mother from whom she'd worked all these years to distance herself.

Ever since her release from prison, her mother had been calling. The calls now came frequently enough that Paisley dreaded looking at her phone.

She regretted having told David her deepest secrets. It wasn't a mistake she'd ever make again.

Even worse? He wasn't even a doctor, but a phlebotomist.

Paisley was too ashamed to tell Monica—or anyone else. Monica would probably post some directive to her fifty-thousand Twitter followers to toilet paper Dr. Dirtbag's house.

A knock on the door jolted her from her sleepy state.

"Come in!" she shouted, praying Wayne would enter and not a random robber.

"You shouldn't leave your door unlocked," Wayne said. Crinkling paper told her he'd set grocery bags on her kitchen counter.

"You shouldn't buy out half the store when you were only going for three items."

"Touché. But I'm hungry, too. Hope you don't mind if I use your grill? Mine died."

"How does a grill die?" Feeling like an upside-down turtle, she struggled to flop over to face him. The apartment's kitchen and living room shared the same space. Another dream was of one day owning her own home, but with Southern California real estate prices, that could be a while. She couldn't wait to decorate to her heart's content with no lease restrictions. Until then, she was stuck with beige walls, carpet and tile. She was at least fortunate to have bought a Christopher Guy sofa and matching armchairs from a client who had deemed them *so last season*.

"I left the grill out. It apparently collapsed from exposure." She watched him rummage around in one of the shopping bags, and then he presented her with a pack of gummy worms. "Hope these are okay? I used to love 'em when I was a kid."

She took one look at the slimy confection and bolted for the restroom. Thankfully, she made it in time, but as she rinsed her mouth and washed her face with a cool washcloth, Paisley found herself reluctant to face Wayne.

"Everything okay in there?" he asked from behind the closed door.

"Sort of."

"Can I help?"

Just thinking about the worms brought a fresh onslaught of nausea. She dashed for the commode.

The door burst open at the worst imaginable time.

"Damn, girl…" Wayne knelt beside her, holding back her coppery hair, rubbing her shoulders, making soothing sounds the way she'd fantasized David would. "How long have you been like this?" He left her to refresh her cool rag, then pressed it to her flushed forehead.

"Forever. I don't mean to sound like a diva, but could I ask you a teensy favor?"

"Anything."

"As soon as humanly possible, could you get those w-worms out of my apartment?"

"Absolutely, but I thought you were craving gummy stuff?"

"Cute bears—that's all. No sharks, either."

"Got it. My bad." He flushed the commode, then took off running for the kitchen.

By the time he returned from disposing of the offensive edible creatures, she'd cleaned herself and once again collapsed on the sofa.

"This is probably going to make me sound like an idiot—" he sat in the armchair opposite her "—but is every pregnant woman this sick?"

"I don't think so. My ob-gyn says this far into my third trimester I should be feeling better—but then she said that about my second trimester, too, so…" She shrugged.

"Well, look…" Leaning forward, he rested his elbows on his knees. "Considering what's going on with you, I'm going to make your soup and my steak, then table my question for another time."

"What question?" She'd forgotten his big mystery. "Whatever it is, you might as well ask. At least it'll take my mind off those disgusting worms."

"Sorry about that." He winced. "I'll grab bears next time I'm out."

"It's okay. I can do it."

"Babe, hate to break it to you, but you're in no condition to do squat. So actually, my proposition could be mutually beneficial."

"But you haven't proposed anything. Spit it out. We've been friends for years. We've discussed work, politics and religion. Surely, this mystery question can't be too bad?"

"Not at all. In fact, once you think about it, it's really no big deal." His crooked grin had her tummy doing happy flips. The man was criminally handsome. "How would you feel about me renting you to be my temporary wife?"

"*What*?" Paisley took a moment for the question to sink in, then bolted for the bathroom.

Chapter Two

"That could've gone better," Wayne mumbled, as he stood outside Paisley's bathroom door. He'd tried letting himself in, but she'd locked it. "Paise?"

"*Go away!*" Her voice might have been muffled, but her tone rang through loud and clear. She thought he was crazy. He'd be first to admit he was, but he hadn't asked her to be his rent-a-wife for himself, but for his dad's dying wish. There was a huge difference. If she'd just let him explain.

"I want to help!"

"You can't—" The sound of her tossing her cookies told him she wasn't naked or anything, so he made a short jog to her kitchen's junk drawer for a safety pin, then picked the bathroom lock.

Sure enough, when he entered, she was back on her knees in front of the commode. Her complexion was gray. Her expression when she glanced his way shattered his heart. He could kill the guy who'd knocked her up, only to abandon her.

Wayne went through his cool washcloth routine again, then sat on the floor behind her. Legs spread, he drew her back to lean against him. His every nurturing instinct, that he usually reserved for horses, had him smoothing her hair back from her forehead, wishing her free of pain.

"I'm so tired," she whispered.

"Sorry."

She waved off his apology. "It's not your fault I was stupid enough to have unprotected sex with a married man."

"I know you well enough—or, at least I think I do—to be sure you wouldn't have been with him if you hadn't loved him and not known about the wife."

"True."

"I saw you kiss him a few times. You seemed happy." The sight of her with another guy initially set Wayne on edge. He and Paisley were friends. He wanted the best for her. Without personally vetting her new guy, Wayne couldn't be sure he was good enough. Clearly, he hadn't been, which pissed off Wayne even more. "How did you find out he was married?"

"After I told him about our baby, he told me he'd pay to have the problem go away."

"Bastard!"

"Right? I told him I'd always wanted to be a mom and have a family. I thought the pregnancy was a surprise blessing. That's when he announced that he and his wife had already been *blessed* three times, and he wasn't interested in having another."

"I assume he's at least paying child support?"

"He said if I promise not to contact him or try talking to his wife, he'll cover labor and delivery costs, but that's it."

Wayne snorted. "I'm no lawyer, but I don't think he gets that choice."

She began crying softly. "H-he made me feel so dirty. Like I'd done something wrong. I—I loved him, but now? I feel empty inside."

"No. You did everything right, hon. Even better? In a few months, you'll have a gorgeous son and all your pig of an ex will have is a child support bill." It ate him up inside to see her so defeated.

"I don't want the legal system involved. As much as I've been hurt, his wife would be devastated to know David had been fooling around. Never in a million years would I have dated a married man. He's scum."

"Agreed. You're too good for him."

"But what about you?" She turned to face him. "What in the world were you talking about earlier? Wanting to *rent* a wife?"

"It was a stupid idea. Sorry I brought it up. I'm especially sorry it upset you enough to make you sick." He grappled to his feet, then knelt, scooping her into his arms.

"I can walk."

"I'm sure you can."

"And it wasn't your bizarre question that made me sick, but thinking about those nasty gummy worms."

He walked down the hall to her bedroom and set her on her unmade bed. After slipping off her pink Converse sneakers, getting her comfy by bunching pillows behind her and under her knees, he drew her floral comforter up to her neck. "Better?"

She nodded.

"I grabbed Sprite at the store. Want some on ice?"

"Yes, please."

He returned to find her asleep.

Not wanting to leave her alone with her door unlocked, he made his steak, then found extreme winter games to watch on ESPN.

By the time he heard stirring from the bedroom, the sun had long since set.

Paisley wandered down the hall. More hair had escaped her ponytail than was in, and her dress looked more like a rumpled prison uniform than her usual classy style. Everything about her kicked Wayne's protective streak into overdrive.

"Let me help you." Up from the sofa, he guided her to where he'd been sitting, then plucked a faux fur throw from the back of the sofa to cover her.

"Thanks, but why are you still here?"

"I don't have a key. What if I'd left you alone and killers or drug dealers strolled inside?"

She rolled her eyes. "Because we have so many of those in our gated community."

"Hey—anything could happen. My job is all about safekeeping our American way of life."

Laughing, she said, "Not to detract from your actual military service, but I've seen you and your buddies protecting—especially bikini models. Yeah…" She winked. "You all kept them super safe."

"I'm serious."

"So am I…" The twinkle in her eyes told him she was not only feeling better, but sassy. It made her kooky hair extra adorable. "Did you ever get my beef jerky?"

"I see how it is—you're just using me for meal delivery?"

"Wayne…" Something about his teasing question served as an instant vibe wrecker. Not a good sign for a guy in serious need of a favor.

He got her snack and poured her another Sprite before sitting across from her and muting the TV. He cleared his throat. "So earlier…"

"When you asked me to be your rental wife?" Eyebrows raised, she shook her head.

"I wasn't going to bring it up again, but since you did, hear me out." Leaning forward, he rested his elbows on his knees. "I haven't told you—or pretty much anyone besides Logan—but my dad has cancer."

"Oh no." She dropped her piece of jerky back into the bag. "Wayne, I'm so sorry. Is he getting treatment?"

"That's just it—he says he's too far gone for that. I've drilled him for more details, but he refuses to talk about it. He doesn't even want Mom to know, but I don't understand how if he's that sick, she hasn't noticed. When I try broaching the subject with her, she tells me he seems tired, but is otherwise fine, Which makes no sense considering his doctors gave him…" His voice cracked with emotion, recalling how much time they'd spent together on the family ranch. It was the little things that now meant so much. Fishing together and building a tree house. The time his junior prom date bailed, so his dad took him camping instead, and told him he could be anything he set his mind to. Even when his marriage crashed and burned, his dad had helped stomp out the fire. "They gave him a couple months to live. He says his sole regret is not having grandkids."

She gasped and covered her mouth, but then hugged her baby bump. "Which is where I come in? You want me to pretend this is your baby? That we're together, so your father rests in peace?" Her gaze welled. "Wayne—that's the sweetest thing ever. But I've met your parents lots of times. Surely they'd remember you and I are just friendly neighbors?"

"Exactly. Think about it. That's what makes this whole plan perfect. What could be more natural than two friends falling for each other and having a baby?"

"Wayne—" She released a long, slow exhale. "You know I love you, but not *that* way."

"That's the best part. I feel the same. You're a great girl, but—"

She frowned. "I'm not your type?"

"I was going to say I'm career military and blow shit up. You, on the other hand, spend your days making the world more beautiful with your design business." Plus, Wayne's divorce left him one hundred percent certain he didn't have the intestinal fortitude to marry again. Give him a bomb over a bombshell of a woman any day. "You're an amazing soul. Any man would be lucky to have you. But this engagement wouldn't be real."

"But what about your mom? She's not dying. What happens when she wants to spend time with the baby after your dad passes?"

"Great question." Now Wayne was the one wearing a frown. "You're right. I hadn't thought that through."

"Although… I suppose after he dies, you could tell her the truth?"

"Does that mean you're at least willing to consider my plan?"

"For you, for your sweet father, of course. But there's a lot involved. We'd have to really be in sync—not just act like friendly neighbors, but…*you know.*" Her blush told him her mind had gone straight to the gutter.

Yeah, he did know.

Once upon a time, a couple weeks after moving in, he'd considered asking Paisley on a date, but then he'd been deployed—hell, maybe a better way of looking at it was that six months in Iraq had given him an overdue reality check. He couldn't put himself through another potential breakup. The pain of loving and losing was too damned intense.

Survival was about keeping his head in the game—not on a woman.

"Thank you." Wayne was caught off guard by the profound gratitude he felt for her in the moment. "It really is a half-baked plan, but…" He worked past the knot in his throat that hardened every time he thought of a world without his father. "If we successfully pull this off and it brings my dad comfort in the last weeks of his life, it could be worth it."

"Absolutely." She wiped silent tears with the backs of her hands.

"This is good." Damned if his eyes weren't also

stinging from the relief of having her onboard. "Nutty-as-a-drunk-squirrel crazy—but good."

"For the record, you have to know this could end in disaster."

"True." But more likely, his plan would bring his father much-needed peace.

"Just to be clear, I refuse to take money. This would strictly be a humanitarian mission."

"Deal." He stood, crossing the short distance between them to shake her hand. Was it his imagination, or was there a spark that had never been there before?

Not cool. Sparks were the last thing he needed from the neighbor he considered one of his best friends.

"Whoa, whoa, whoa. Back up the truck." In the glorified closet that served as Velvet's break room, Monica tossed her usual frozen breakfast burrito in the microwave, then slammed the door before setting the time. "Wayne—hotshot, abs-of-steel navy SEAL—wants to *rent* you and your unborn baby? Sweetie…" She shook her head. "That's more than a little twisted."

As if on cue, Paisley's cell buzzed. Her mother. One more problem she'd prefer avoiding. Paisley touched the decline button for the call.

"You can't keep this up forever. One day, you will have to talk to your mom."

"I don't doubt that for a second, but that day isn't this day. Now, where were we?"

"You were trying rather unsuccessfully to explain why you're agreeing to Wayne's crazy scheme."

"His dad is dying." While Monica ate her smelly

meal, Paisley struggled not to retch as she relayed pertinent details. "With all of that in mind, how could I turn him down?"

"Gee—did it ever occur to you to just say no?"

"Well, sure, but then he looked so sad, and—"

"The man's no doubt been trained in psychological warfare. Playing dirty was the only way Logan got me to date him."

"Let's be real—Logan's ass in a pair of jeans worked most of his magic."

"Language!" Monica scolded. "You're about to be a mother."

"And if you for one second pretend you weren't just as hot for Logan as he was for you, then you're a liar."

"All right. What can I say? The guy has it going on. But he also thinks *commitment* is a four-letter word. Besides, my dad would never approve."

"Wait—" Eyebrows raised, Paisley leaned across the table. "Are you saying that if Logan proposed and Daddy Conrad actually approved, you might still be together?"

Monica chewed extra fast before swallowing, then said, "I'm not sure how you turned this issue around on me, but it's not going to work. The matter at hand is the fact that Wayne is using you. Sweetie, you've got the biggest heart of anyone I've ever known, but you also have a seriously full plate. You're a business owner on the verge of becoming a single mom. You have about two free hours a day when you're not puking your guts out, and I selfishly need you to spend them here."

Paisley drew her lower lip into her mouth for a nibble.

"Oh God..." Monica fisted her burrito's plastic wrapper. "You already told him you'd do it."

Nodding, shaking her head, Paisley settled for a shrug. "What can I say? Rampant pregnancy hormones made me a sucker for his sad, stormy-gray eyes—but it's all good. We were both up front about this being a platonic, temporary humanitarian gig."

"Lord... In the immortal words of Cher, 'Snap out of it!' This man is not your friend. He's a neighbor who doesn't need a simple cup of sugar, but your womb. There's no way you'll fool his dad, let alone his mother. The whole plan is ludicrous."

True. *So why does my heart skip a beat every time I think about getting started?*

Chapter Three

Over a week later, Paisley dropped the kitchen window's curtain. The last thing she needed was for Wayne to catch her spying.

Was it her imagination, or had he been to the communal Dumpster more in the past thirty minutes than he had for the past few months? If so, what did his actions mean? Was he also still confused by their last conversation?

She was so deep in thought that when a knock sounded on the front door, she was nearly startled into a premature delivery. A peek through the eyehole landed her face-to-face with the man she'd been practically stalking. Had he caught her?

"Hey. What's up?" She strove for a breezy, nonstalker tone.

"Not much." He leaned against her doorjamb. Was he also trying a little too hard to look carefree? "It's a, um, gorgeous day. Want to stroll the duck pond?"

"I suppose that would be okay. Let me find shoes."

"Sure. Take all the time you need."

She hated the awkwardness between them. Before

his "proposal," they'd been chill. Friends. Now? She couldn't read his vibe, but knew him well enough to recognize it wasn't normal.

When her shoes didn't show up in any convenient places, she dropped to her knees to search under the sofa. No luck.

It took a mortifying three times to push and grunt her way back onto her feet. Even then, she wasn't especially steady.

"Whoa." Wayne grabbed her arm. "Take it easy."

"Thanks. I get dizzy if I stand too fast—which seems silly since it takes me forever to stand."

"I'm in no hurry. The CO had to be home early tonight for his daughter's choir concert. His wife insisted. But hey, his family drama is my gain." His crooked grin should have been endearing, but Paisley was mortified by his comment.

"How do you consider something as sweet as a mother wanting her daughter's father to see their child sing to be drama?"

"I was teasing. Logan says the CO's wife gets bent out of shape if he's so much as a minute late—kinda like how he goes off on us."

"It wasn't funny." Where were her stupid sandals?

"Why are you so testy?"

"Why shouldn't I be? You fake proposed to me, the clock's ticking on us becoming a convincing couple by Easter weekend, yet I haven't seen you in days."

"Sorry. Work's been hell on a stick." He fished her sandal out from under the kitchen table, then asked,

"I am curious, though. What kinds of plans have you dreamed up?"

"After all this bickering, I'm no longer in the mood to tell you. Besides…" she rubbed her burning chest "…now I have wicked indigestion."

He landed her sandal on the coffee table. "What can I do to help? Need medicine?"

"I wish, but I'm doing an all-natural pregnancy." She rubbed her throat, too, then winced. "It's really bad."

"There has to be something you can do?"

She nodded before dropping to the sofa. "But it would take too much effort."

"Name it. Whatever it is, I'll get it done."

"Thanks—if you're sure it's not too much trouble, I need a tablespoon of honey dissolved into a cup of warm milk."

"Those exact measurements?" As if she'd sent him on a life-or-death mission, he was already halfway to the kitchen.

"Close is fine."

"Got it."

While he banged pots, Paisley warred with her conscience. She had to admit, having Wayne around more often wouldn't be a terrible thing. On the flip side, as a soon-to-be single mom, she needed to learn to be independent. Leaning on Wayne, only to lose him when he no longer needed her, would do her or her baby no good.

Eyes closed, she willed her heart rate to slow.

What was wrong with her?

Being around Wayne had never caused this sort of indescribable, system-wide panic. They were friends.

Why was she now concerned if he was judging her for not having done the dishes or wiped down her stove? Did rough-and-tough guys like him even look at stuff like that? Cerebral Dr. Dirtbag had, but his opinion no longer mattered.

"Almost done," Wayne called out.

"Thanks."

A few minutes longer than it had taken her to nibble what little remained of her fingernails, he handed her a steaming mug. Their fingers brushed during the exchange, resulting in still more confusion. Butterflies flapped up a storm in her tummy. That was new. "Careful. It's hot."

"Bless you." The soothing liquid proved perfect. After a few sips, she could have purred with relief.

"Well?" Instead of resuming his seat opposite her, he perched beside her on the couch. "What's on your mind?"

She worried her lower lip. "I'm one hundred percent ready to help, but I do have reservations."

"Shoot."

Did he have to sit close enough for his radiant heat to warm her chilly toes? It was distracting her from sharing concerns—of which there were plenty!

"Okay…" She licked her lips. "First, I think we should let your mom in on our secret."

"Out of the question."

"Why?"

"Because I love her dearly, but she's incapable of keeping a secret. For Dad to genuinely believe I'm going to be a father, I'm sorry, but Mom also should believe. We'll break the news to her after Dad passes."

"What if I have the baby before then?"

"I'll consider myself blessed." He sighed. Scratched his forehead. "There's no delicate way to say this, so I'll blurt it out. Dad is dying. He may have a couple months, but according to his doctors, we're only looking at weeks."

Paisley caught herself holding her breath. "That's so sad."

"Agreed. And look, I know this whole idea is FUBAR, but—"

Nose wrinkled, she asked, "What's that?"

"Military slang that shouldn't be used in the presence of ladies. Basically, it just means our pretending to be married is about as screwed up as anything we could ever do, but for the sake of my dad, we're only talking about maintaining this act for sixty days—ninety tops. When are you due?"

"Eighty-eight days." She hugged her baby bump. "Please don't take this the wrong way, but if your father should pass before then, I think news of this charade would be easier on your mom. If I have my baby and she grows attached to him, believing he's her grandson, that could hurt her more."

"True. It's a potential minefield all the way around. But I'm looking at risk versus reward. I can't stomach the thought of Dad passing with regrets."

"Have you ever thought to consider that this news might be so agreeable to your father that it actually helps him recover? Miracles might be rare with his kind of disease, but I'm sure they do happen. What are we going to do if he's so thrilled with our sham marriage that he goes into remission?"

Eyebrows furrowed, Wayne asked, "I fail to see how this is a problem? That would be awesome."

"Not if the whole reason for his recovery is an eight-pound bundle of joy who isn't his grandson."

"Oh." His shoulders sagged. "I see what you mean. But hey—that's a long shot. I promise, if something like that happens, I'll take the heat. You won't even have to be there when I come clean."

"Promise?"

"Absolutely."

"Okay…"

"Does that mean you'll still do it?"

"I already said I would." Monica would lecture her till the end of time about the recklessness and irresponsibility of this plan, but since when had her fun-loving business partner and best friend become the morality police?

"You're awesome." Wayne stood, only to then kneel beside her, squeezing her in an awkward, but not entirely awful, hug. "You won't regret this. I'll map out the whole thing. Oh—and we'll need wedding pics."

"What?" Her indigestion roared back.

"Relax. You can help me find a suitable thrift shop gown."

"Do you have any idea how hard it would be to find one my current size?"

"No worries…" Rocking back on his heels, his slow sideways grin disarmed her. "We'll grab a dress in a style you like, then chop it off midway down. It'll be perfect for a few head-only selfies."

Paisley groaned.

Why had Wayne ruined his temporary charm by being an idiot?

Two DAYS LATER, Paisley found herself not buying part of a dress, but on her way to a bakery. Being next to him in the cab of his truck was too close for rational thought. Besides looking extra hot in his cowboy hat and Ray-Ban Aviators, he smelled too good—like the beach and a great deli. Had he recently eaten? She wouldn't mind eating. "Do we really need a wedding cake? Seems like overkill."

"Yeah. We'll have that classic wedding shot where we're shoving cake in each other's mouths."

"Mmm… Sounds romantic."

"You know what I mean. Lion—one of my teammates—recommended the place where we're headed, but then his wedding got canceled—long story. They specialize in fake cakes. Super cheap, but totally legit looking."

Her only comment was to raise her eyebrows, then shake her head. She turned her gaze from him to the scenery outside her window.

"Tell me you don't love a bargain."

"Of course, I do, but this— Never mind."

"What?"

"Nothing."

He made a left. "God, I hate when women pull this crap."

"I'm not pulling anything."

"The hell you're not. You're pissed about something, but won't say it. Instead, you're taking the passive aggressive approach which—"

"Am not."

"Are, too."

"Am—" Her cell rang. Rather than continue their argument, she answered. "Hey."

"Are you alone?" Even though the phone wasn't on speaker, Monica's voice rang through loud and clear.

"No."

"Still stuck with the pretend fiancé?"

"Uh-huh."

"Okay, well, sorry. But I have a major crisis and need your advice."

"Is something wrong at the shop? Or with a client?"

"No, no. Nothing like that. Logan called. He wants to meet for coffee. He doesn't even drink coffee, but knows I love that cute place on the corner that has the great patio and garden."

"How is this a bad?"

"Because I don't know what to say. Or wear. The last time we were together, we both said some harsh things, and—"

Paisley sighed. "Monica, talk to him. What's the worst that can happen?"

"I end up sleeping with him and falling hard all over again? Worse—we break up again."

"Point of fact—I'm pretty sure you never fully let go of him, and second, how many times have I heard you brag about his superhero bedroom talents?"

Paisley glanced at Wayne and saw him smirking.

"Of course, I'm over him. I hate him. And his stupid dimples. And the way he fills out that pair of designer jeans I bought him, but he claims to—"

"Monica, I have to go. I'm going to be sick." Paisley ended the call.

"Do I NEED to pull over?" Wayne asked, worrying equal amounts for his leather upholstery and her.

"Nope. I'm fine. But Monica's constant whining about Logan pisses me off. How can she not see how great they are together? What even happened to break them up?"

"No clue. Although Logan did mention something about having talked with her dad." He pulled into the bakery's crowded lot. The white brick structure featured pink-and-white-striped awnings. The Cake Place was written over the entry in hot pink neon script. "Think this place sells doughnuts?"

"Maybe?" In all the years they'd known each other, he'd never seen her so snippy. Especially with her best friend.

"Please tell me what's got you in a mood."

"It's lame."

Progress? At least she was admitting there was a problem.

"Worse than Logan and Monica pretending they're not insanely hot for each other?"

She laughed. "This is stupid, but you hurt my feelings."

"What did I do?" He killed the engine, removed the keys, then turned to face her.

She worried her lower lip. "More what you didn't do. But now that I've had time to reflect, I'm making a big deal out of nothing and you're forgiven." After opening her door, she eased out of the truck and onto her feet.

"Oh no—" He gave chase. "You're not getting off that easy. Tell me your beef."

"Leave it alone. Sorry I said anything." She entered the bakery, zeroing in on a wedding cake display.

"May I help you?" a clerk asked.

"We need a simple wedding cake," Paisley said.

"How many guests will you be expecting?"

"Just the two of us. I mainly want it for our wedding album—something special to commemorate the occasion."

"Of course." The clerk's name tag read Daisy. "But an option many of our brides choose is our fake cake."

"Perfect," Wayne said. "I heard about them."

Paisley's furrowed brow read confusion. "I'm not sure about this."

Daisy laughed, leading them to a corner display. She plucked up a seriously swanky, three-tiered cake, tossing it to Wayne. "Catch."

He did, bracing for the impact of fifty pounds' worth of cake and frosting. Instead, the thing must have been made of Styrofoam and couldn't weigh over five pounds. "Impressive."

"I know, right? We're famous for them and ship worldwide. Our fake cakes have been featured on hundreds of feature films and TV programs. We even make simple sheet cakes for your guests to enjoy, but if you choose to buy rather than rent, your wedding cake can be the perfect keepsake of your special day."

"Sold," Wayne said. What could be better for a fake marriage than a fake cake? He turned to his betrothed. "Pick which one you want. Maybe it's my affinity for all things Western, but I'm vibing on the one with all those little cacti and the cowboy hat topper." To Daisy he asked, "Do you rent by the hour? We just need it for pics. Oh, and we'll need one piece of real cake to smoosh in each other's faces."

"Perfect. We do rent by the hour, and there's an adorable park just at the end of the street with a rose garden perfect for photos. For an additional fee, we can set the cake on a banquet table and even take professional photos. We call this our Social Media Wedding Package. It has all the panache of a spectacular wedding event for the price of dinner and a movie. We can also handle your floral needs—arrangements, bouquet and boutonnieres—the works. They're made from the finest silks and trust me, from photos they look real enough to smell. Your friends and family will be impressed."

"Sign us up."

"Wayne," Paisley said, "isn't this all moving a little fast? Plus, I think your mom will be less disappointed to have missed our wedding if we make it a simple, courthouse ceremony. Frills will only upset her."

"Relax. Considering we have to be married and on the family ranch with photo proof by Easter, which is in only three weeks, this is the perfect solution. And I think Mom would be more disappointed if I didn't treat my bride to a good time. She'll understand that because of the baby, we needed a rush job."

Paisley's thunderous expression said she wasn't so sure.

Back in the truck, before he started the engine, he angled sideways to face her. "So, what's bugging you? And don't tell me nothing, because we shouldn't be lying this soon into our relationship." He winked, trying to keep things light.

"Honestly? Besides your faulty rationale in regard to your sweet mother's potentially broken heart?" She gazed out her window rather than at him. "It may sound stupid, but I'd like more regular communication between us. You go days without so much as a text, then pop in unannounced. Even as your pretend fiancée, I'd appreciate more consideration. I don't expect a full accounting of your every move, but regular updates would be great."

"Noted." Interesting. One part of him was annoyed by having to check in. Another part was flattered she cared…

Chapter Four

"What's got you so damned smiley?" Wayne was hating every second of their 0500 six-mile beach run. A three-mile ocean swim was next on the PT agenda. Most days he didn't mind, but ever since learning of his father's condition, he felt as if his time would be better spent on the ranch.

"You probably wouldn't believe me if I told you. Hell—I still don't believe it."

"Knock off the chitchat!" Their CO passed them as if they were standing still. "You losers aren't a SEAL team, but freakin' cheerleading squad. Move it, move it, *move!*"

"Such a charmer," Logan said once their commanding officer passed them to harass the next guys in line. "But not even his hard ass could bring me down. You're not the only one around here getting married—only mine's the real deal."

"Wait—*what?*"

"You heard me. I popped the question to Monica last night and she accepted. She wanted me to ask if you'd mind us tagging along to your family ranch. We want to get hitched over Easter. No big deal. I'm sure your dad isn't up for a major production. But since that's the only leave we have coming for a while and I want you to be my best man and Monica wants Paisley for her maid of honor, it makes sense."

"No, man. Nothing about this makes sense. You hate Monica. She hates you. My dad's dying. Like seriously, what the hell?"

"What can I say? We kissed and made up. And I couldn't be happier. Not only is Monica obsessed with the photos I've shown her of your family ranch, but your dad has always been like a second father to me. Your mom, like my mom." Tears shone in Logan's eyes. He swiped them away. "Since my mother passed, they've been there for me. It would mean a lot for them to share this special day—especially, since your dad is—well, since he's not feeling his best."

"I appreciate all that, but I thought you had that ugly talk with her father?"

"It wasn't so much ugly as it was a gut check. He basically asked my intentions. When I told him we were having a good time, he told me she was ready for a more serious commitment. He also told me not to even think about seeing his daughter anymore unless I was one thousand percent ready for a lifelong marriage. I got spooked and broke things off. But damned if being without her didn't scare me more than being with her. I missed her, you know?"

"You've lost your ever-loving mind."

"Is that a yes for the ranch? I showed Monica pics from the last time we were there and she couldn't get enough of those back-porch views. Oh—and Monica told me your fake wedding is right before we leave. I'm hurt you didn't ask me to stand up for you."

"You're an idiot."

"Nah." Logan flashed a smile. "Just a fool for love. By the way, I ran this past your mom and she loves the idea—although she's crushed you and Paisley aren't joining us for a double wedding. Monica and I both think you should reconsider."

Hours later, Wayne was fresh out of the shower when his cell rang. Caller ID showed his mom, so he answered. "Hey. Is Dad all right?"

All he heard was her crying. The sound wrung his heart like a soaked towel.

"Mom? Is Dad having a rough day?"

"H-how could you do this to me? Y-you're my only son! Y-you not only got that sweet neighbor of yours p-pregnant, but couldn't bother to tell us y-you're getting married again?"

Lord…

Think fast. "Mom, I'm sorry. I thought with everything going on with Dad—the divorce from Chelsea—it would be better to just—"

"When is it ever an appropriate time to break your mother's heart? Logan told me you and Paisley aren't married yet, so I worked everything out with Monica's wedding planner and we're having a nice double wedding. It's happening on a whirlwind timeline, but I'm excited. This is all going to be a lot of fun. I can only imagine the cost."

"*What?*" Raging heartburn had the protein bar he'd

downed doing push-ups in his stomach. Like the entire world wasn't shattering, he covered his right ear from the sound of guys laughing in the showers.

"Son?"

"Dad?" Wayne gulped. "How are you feeling?"

"Fine. Fine. Like new man. This news has me happier than June bug dancing in lemonade. I'm finally going to be grandpoppa!" Wayne would miss his Russian-born father's thick accent and ridiculous analogies that rarely, if ever, made sense, but somehow still managed to convey his meaning. At least he was happy, which was fantastic.

But only if he and Paisley pulled off their charade. He could only imagine what Monica's nickname for them would be.

#Payne?

The joining of his and Paisley's names would be hilarious if not so tragic.

"Wayne? It's Mom." *Swell.* "The double wedding will be lovely. The thought of it is the only thing stopping me from permanently grounding you."

"But, Mom—"

"Not another word. You and Paisley are getting married here and that's final. Pastor Jim will perform the ceremony, and I'll trust you to have the license and ring."

Before he could tell her no, she hung up. Great.

What was he going to tell Paisley? Damn Logan and Monica. This was all their fault.

Not entirely.

His father's disease was the true culprit.

Was his mother so overwrought with the realization of losing her husband that she wasn't thinking straight? While tending to his medical needs, there was no way she could handle one wedding, let alone two. What if the added stress made her sick?

On the flip side, his dad had never sounded better. His normally pitiful tone boomed with what Wayne could only guess was anticipation.

But how was he supposed to pull off a fake marriage with a real pastor and marriage license? Suddenly, for a man who'd spent his entire adult life training for impossible missions, Wayne found himself in the untenable situation of being in way over his head.

"IT WAS SO SWEET." Monica practically floated to unlock the shop door. "Logan thought of everything. He hired a mariachi band and had the lead singer present my ring. My Instagram followers went wild."

"You hate mariachi bands," Paisley said on her way into her office. Since learning of her best friend's sudden engagement, she'd been downing gummy bears by the fistfuls, and needed the emergency stash she had hidden in her desk's bottom right drawer.

"This one was different. Incredibly special. *Eek!* Can you believe I'm getting married?"

"Not really." Bears in hand, Paisley rejoined Monica in the shop's showroom. "Just yesterday, you despised Logan. What changed?" And why couldn't Paisley shake the deep sadness stemming from the fear that she'd never sport an engagement ring. She didn't even have a fake one.

Her cell rang. Since it was her mom, she hit Decline.
Monica cocked her head and frowned.

Paisley wished for a decline button for her friend's
disapproval.

"Anyway," Monica said, "I could never hate Logan.
But I won't lie that he hurt my feelings when Daddy
asked his intentions toward me and Logan broke up.
When he explained that he'd been scared, I totally un-
derstood. And now…" She collapsed onto her desk chair
with a happy sigh. "We're getting married!"

"You already told me. Like fourteen times."

"Sorry. I'm *really* excited. Oh—and here's the best
part. I guess Logan is close with Wayne's family and
we're going with you and Wayne over Easter. I've always thought one of those barn weddings would be
adorable. Anyway, Logan worked it out with Wayne's
mom—promised her she wouldn't have to lift a finger
aside from eating cake and drinking champagne. Of
course, you'll be my maid of honor and Wayne will
be Logan's best man. It's going to be perfect. I already
hired a wedding planner, and he'll handle every detail
superfast. All we have to do is show up."

Paisley knew she should be thrilled for her friend.
And she wanted to be. Really. But beyond the insanity
of this one-eighty regarding Monica and Logan's crazy
relationship, what about Wayne's father?

Paisley cleared her throat. "Is Wayne's dad healthy
enough for a big wedding?"

"I guess? Logan asked Wayne's mom and she said
that aside from the arthritis in his knees, he's feeling
fine. Of course, I asked Logan not to specifically bring

up the cancer. She must be out of her mind with worry. Who knows? Maybe the joy of Easter combined with our ceremony and the news that she and Peter are going to be grandparents will send Peter straight into remission?"

Paisley sat down hard on one of Monica's acrylic desk chairs. "You're going to send me into early labor. Wayne and I planned to surprise his parents with our news."

"Oops. Sorry. Want me to call her back? I could ask her to act surprised?"

"Stop." Paisley pressed her fingers to her forehead. Just when she thought her life couldn't get worse, it nose-dived to a whole new level of disaster.

AFTER AN ENDLESS day of statuary shopping and paint selection for Mickey and Rick Levy's formal entry hall remodel, Paisley drove home. *Exhaustion* didn't come close to describing her level of tired. Her feet throbbed. Her lower back ached, and her boobs had mysteriously swollen to twice the normal size.

She'd just dumped split pea soup in a pan to boil, then headed to her room to change into sweatpants and a roomy T-shirt when a knock sounded on her door. Wayne? Part of her hoped it was him, but another part just wanted to be left alone. In the face of Monica and Logan's true commitment, Paisley's sham marriage felt icky and wrong.

A look through the peephole showed Wayne standing outside.

The baby kicked. Was that a good or bad sign?

Rubbing her belly with one hand, she opened the door with her other. "Are you as sick of hashtag *#Mogan* as I am?"

Wayne groaned. "As part of my best man duties, Logan made me put on a T-shirt that read SEALing the Deal! *#Mogan*."

"Eew. I have no doubt I'd have been in the same boat, only Monica couldn't find a T-shirt big enough to fit over my belly."

He laughed, then drew her into a welcome hug. "Sorry. That wasn't funny. For the record, I think your bump is cute."

"Thanks?" It should be criminal for a man to smell so good. Hints of sweat, sun and Irish Spring wrapped her in the cozy bliss of Wayne's strong arms. If she were smart, she'd resist, pushing against him until reaching a safe distance that allowed her to think. This close, her only coherent thought was that she could stay like this forever. Which totally wasn't happening, so she ushered him inside and shut the door before checking on her soup. "I should be scolding you popping in again unannounced, but we have bigger issues. What are you thinking for damage control? I guess the happy couple already told your mom we're getting married and expecting."

"Well…" He sighed, helping himself to her fridge. "You've gotta get more food."

"I'd love to—assuming the baby follows this trend of actually allowing me to eat."

"Right." He shut the fridge door.

"Want some of my soup?"

He blanched.

"Okay, spill it," Paisley said.

"Your soup?"

Hands on her hips, she frowned. "*Really?* Spill the reason why your complexion looks grayer than mine."

He sighed. "You're not going to like it. I don't like it. Honestly? We should bail."

"Is this about *#Mogan*?" She poured her soup into a mug, then joined him at her kitchen table that was a repurposed wrought iron patio set she'd painted white. Her protruding belly wouldn't allow her anywhere near the table's surface, so she cradled her mug and leaned back in her chair.

"Look, I don't know any way to say this other than blurting it. My mom called and is expecting us to get married along with the happy couple. She's arranged for our family pastor to perform the service and told me to show up with you and our license. She's expecting a real marriage, but we—"

"Are *just* neighbors! What do you mean we're getting married? Like she's expecting a *real* wedding in front of God and everyone we know? It's official, you've gone off the deep end. I don't even have a dress."

"We'll find one."

She rolled her eyes.

"Promise, everything will be fine. Besides, as soon as Dad . . . Well, we both know this is only temporary."

The fact made her beyond sad.

But it was the truth.

Another truth? The more this sham relationship forced the two of them together, the more she saw that maybe Wayne was more of a stand-up guy than she'd always thought. He was handsome and sensitive. Funny. A safe driver. Great for fishing her flip-flops out from under her sofa. But legit husband material? Nope. Not happening. Her baby boy was all the testosterone she could handle.

For his dad, for the sake of their friendship, she had to play this sham marriage through to the tragic end.

"I've got an idea." She set her mug on the table.

"Lay it on me."

"What if we faked the license? I'm sure we can grab one online, then fill it out, but not file it. For that matter, you could even grab a legit one from the courthouse."

Eyebrows raised, he asked, "You'd be okay with lying before our friends, my family and God?"

"How upset was your mother?"

"Sobbing. I've never heard her like that. But she wasn't upset about Dad—but us. She was mad at me. I honestly don't think she has a clue how bad off he is. Which means he's either doing a miraculous job of hiding it from her, or there's more to the story. She wouldn't even talk about him. It was bizarre. But then he got on the phone and sounded happier than I've ever heard him. He was a new man. Didn't even sound sick."

"Grief affects everyone differently."

"I suppose."

"Or, maybe you're right and he hasn't told her. I can't imagine how tough it would be for him to hide something like this, but I suppose if he's determined it could be done. We won't know for sure until we get there and see the two of them together."

Arching his neck, he rubbed his eyes with his thumb and forefingers. "I'm sorry to have dragged you into this. We should probably call it off. I'll come clean with my parents and—"

"No way. If this news made such a huge improvement in your dad's entire demeanor, we should at least try. If he makes a full recovery and they figure out our marriage isn't legit, we'll deal with it then, but otherwise, for his sake, let's roll with it."

"You're sure?" He held his hand out to her, only not to shake, but hold.

Her pulse quickened at his touch. Her attraction to her neighbor had Paisley unsure of her own name, let alone if this was a good or bad decision. But then he released her and she just as quickly rationalized this was a horrible decision—for her.

For Wayne's poor, dying dad? It was the only way to go.

Paisley nodded. "Absolutely. Let's do this."

THE FRIDAY BEFORE the Easter weekend, after a grueling run and ocean swim, Wayne brushed sand from his base locker, beyond relieved for the weekend and to get off at the highly reasonable hour of 3:00 p.m.

He'd worked it out with his CO to have a week's leave in conjunction with the Easter holiday. Logan had done the same. The plan was to leave next Thursday, celebrate and help with wedding prep, get married on Saturday, celebrate Easter Sunday, then depart for a brief honeymoon at some nearby swanky ranch/spa that Monica's mother highly recommended.

Wayne was exhausted just thinking about it all. He hated lying to his parents. But then he remembered the way his father had brightened at the news of the wedding and baby. It had been downright miraculous.

Logan approached, swatting Wayne's ass with his towel.

"What the hell?" Wayne snapped. He was already on edge from the angry rock one of the younger guys was playing at full blast at the other end of the room.

"Chill, bro. I'm high on life. God, I can't wait to be married. Monica decided we'll be living at her place for the time being, but her folks want to buy us a house for a wedding gift. Can you believe it? Am I the luckiest guy on earth, or what?"

"I'm happy for you," Wayne said. "If you're sure this is what you want?"

"Of course, it is. I love her, she loves me. Done deal."

Logan dropped his towel to pull on boxers.

Wayne returned to his locker; he'd brushed and brushed, but there always seemed to be more sand. Story of his life.

"Are you and Baby Momma getting hitched for real?"

"Don't call her that," Wayne said with an angry crackle to his tone. "And no. After my last go-round with marriage, I'm never doing it again. We'll fake the license. I'll talk with Pastor Jim at the rehearsal— explain about Dad."

Logan whistled. "That sounds fun."

"Screw you. It never would have gone this far if you

and Monica hadn't invited yourselves to what would have otherwise been an ordinary weekend."

"Keep telling yourself that, buddy." Logan slapped his shoulder. "You were drowning in this from the first day you popped the question to your girl."

"She's not my girl and you started this whole thing by suggesting I rent a wife."

Laughing, Logan said, "I didn't know you'd be stupid enough to actually do it."

"Yo—how come no one else is invited to your weddings?" Lion wandered up. Big, blond and sometimes scary, Lion had been given his call sign for his tendency to roar when going into battle. Plus, his furrowed brows made him look perma-pissed.

"Agreed." Monk was next in the complaint line. His name came from his preference to hole up with his Bible during leave as opposed to hitting bars. He kept his hair buzzed so short that no one remembered the shade other than buzz-black. "Friends don't let friends hit an open bar alone."

"Since when do you even drink?" Logan asked Monk.

"I drink plenty—only, since I stick with fine wines, none of you beer guzzlers ever see it."

The room erupted in laughs.

Wayne slammed his locker door, escaping the crowd to let Logan handle the mess he'd created.

Outside in the blazing sun, he gulped fresh air.

The worst part of this whole thing was that the more he was around Paisley, the more he enjoyed her company. She was a good woman. Sweet and funny. Cute and yet still somehow sexy. She was the kind of total package that if he had been looking, he might be interested in catching. But he wasn't. He couldn't. He had his career to consider. His dying father. His mother.

Plus, he'd already tried marriage once and it was a complete failure.

In his truck, he didn't just drive to his apartment complex, but to Paisley. For some odd reason, he craved being with her. Getting to know her. He wasn't typically a touchy-feely guy, but for once, considering what he was going through with his dad, he'd go with it.

With her.

Chapter Five

"Wayne." Paisley stood at the partially open door wearing a voluminous pink sundress. With her hair in pigtails, she probably looked twelve—not counting her baby bump. "You're the last person I expected to see. What happened to you calling first before popping in?"

"What kind of welcome is that for your fiancé?"

"Ha-ha. Look, it's really not—"

He brushed past her to pace her living room. He was so large that his constant motion cramped the already tight space. "I was thinking…"

"Yes?" She closed the door, then collapsed onto the sofa.

"It occurred to me…"

That you should call before barging in on a woman who is wearing her fave grunge wear?

"You and I are pretending to be engaged. We leave next week for our wedding, yet have never been on a date. Wanna go?"

"Now?" She fingered her dress that was more of a nightgown. "I'm not exactly…"

"You look adorable. Let's go." He took her hands,

tugging her from the sofa. "There are a couple of things you need to go along with that perfect wedding gown we've still got to find you."

"What else do I need?" Was it wrong that even though she felt perfectly stable she didn't want to let go of his hands?

"It's a surprise." Sadly, he released her to fish under the chair. "Go ahead and put these on." He set her sandals in front of her to step into. How did he always seem to know right where to find them? The brush of his fingertips against her ankles made her happy she'd shaved last night in the tub. His touch made her a little dizzy. A little too excited to go anywhere he wanted. A little less determined than she should have been to guard her battered heart. "You'll also need a nice, thick pair of socks."

"Why?"

"If I told you, it wouldn't be a surprise." He grinned.

She wanted to keep a straight face. She wanted to not get suckered by his lone dimple or strong white teeth or perfectly sun-kissed tan. But she couldn't. Her lips curved into a matching grin, and then she succumbed to the excitement of her first happy surprise in a long, long time.

It wasn't until she sat beside Wayne in his truck, stealing a glance at his chiseled profile and dashing cowboy hat and strong forearms gripping the wheel, that it occurred to her the last time she'd fallen for a guy, she'd ended up pregnant and alone.

Before she went and did something idiotic like falling for her fake fiancé, maybe it was time she told him to turn around? To take her home. Where she'd be safely tucked away from his mesmerizing slow grin and the sexy scent of Irish Spring. Most of all, she needed to guard her heart from the way he made her feel.

Protected. Sheltered. Needed.

Emotional ambrosia for a woman in her condition.

A ticking bomb preordained to explode the moment he no longer had a practical use for her in his life.

IN A MILLION YEARS, Wayne never could've envisioned himself easing a sock up a pregnant woman's silky calf, but here he was, literally kneeling at Paisley's feet in the center of Boot Bonanza. "Above all, when picking a new pair of boots, you should opt for comfort. All these flashy designs look nice in the store, but when you're twenty miles down a box canyon, searching for a lost calf, trust me, comfort's gonna win every time."

Paisley cocked her head, eyeing him funny.

"I'm serious."

"I know. And it means the world to me that you want my feet well protected, but let's think this through. I'm an interior designer who lives in San Diego and will soon have a bouncing baby boy. When do you think I'll find time to traipse through box canyons?"

"You know what I mean. And since when is it wrong for a guy to want to look out for you?"

"Never. Thank you. Just sayin' that the majority of shoes in my closet were chosen for form over function."

"That may well be, but on my watch, I think you should be in more stable footwear. Those sandals you wear are totally unsuitable for a woman in your condition. Did you know 35 percent of women reported falling at least two or more times during pregnancy?"

She scrunched her adorable button nose. "Where did you hear that?"

"Internet." He pushed a roomy, brown leather boot onto her left foot.

"Oh—well, then you know it's true." She winked.

"I don't appreciate your sass. This is important."

"I know. Thank you. Really. I've never thought of myself as a Western-wear girl, but these are fun." She stuck out her legs and wriggled her feet.

"Fun has nothing to do with comfort. Let's get you up and walking around." When he reached over to help her up, the feel of her hand in his felt right. When it came to Paisley, something about her made him not want to let go. But he did. Then took it a step further by wiping his palms on his jeans.

He needed a reminder not to get used to having her around. This was strictly a temporary gig.

Her purse hummed. "Is that your cell?"

She took one look at it, hit Decline, then shoved it back into the depths of her bag.

"I don't mind you taking a call."

"It's not important." She peered at her feet, then up at him with a smile so bright, so filled with silly wonder over a pair of cowboy boots, that he smiled, too. "Hate to admit it, but these are great. I feel so stable— imagine that?"

"Told you. Now we need to find a hat."

"Really? I don't want to look like I'm trying too hard. Won't it seem…touristy? Like I'm a poser?"

He pointed to his own trusty hat. "Do I look like a poser?"

"No. But you grew up on a ranch. I spent my formative years in a crap apartment in Anaheim."

"Doesn't matter. My dad always says being a cowboy is more of a state of mind than way of life. Don't get me wrong—having a few acres and a horse sure wouldn't hurt your cowgirl street cred, but you've already got the good stuff. Loyalty. Honor. A dedication to always doing your best. You're not afraid of challenging work."

"You could be describing a golden retriever."

He rolled his eyes. "Whatever. Quit busting my balls. I'm being serious."

"So am I." When she followed her quick grin with a wink, his pulse revved. Was his fake fiancée flirting? Was it wrong that, if so, he liked it? If this sort of thing continued, he could see it being a problem. How the hell was a guy supposed to steer clear of a woman he was starting to enjoy being with damn near as much as his horse?

"You look awfully good in that hat." Wayne fixed Paisley with such a surprisingly intense stare that her cheeks warmed.

"Thanks." She ducked her gaze. "Guess this is the one?" She'd tried on at least a dozen cowboy hats that hadn't done much for her, but this one made her look adventurous. Maybe even a little mysterious. Even sexy? At that, she couldn't help but smile.

"What's that about?" Wayne grinned back.

"No clue what you mean." Monica was always talking about her womanly power. Was this what she'd been referring to? The feeling that she was invincible in the face of any man? Too bad because even though the notion had been fun, even empowering, Paisley wasn't in the market for romance. After what happened with Dr. Dirtbag, she wasn't even sure she still believed in romance. Maybe it was a convention created solely for selling greeting cards, candy and flowers?

"Uh-oh." Wayne's smile faded. "Now what's going on in that pretty head? I swear you have more mood changes than my CO. He's just plain mean. What's your excuse?"

She took off the hat and hugged it to her chest. "How come you've never been in a long-term relationship?"

"How do you know I haven't?" He took the box with her boots, then aimed for the checkout.

She followed. "I guess I just assumed."

"You know what they say about assumptions?"

"No?" They were next in line. Since there was a family with three small kids in front of them and the old saying about assuming making an ass out of you and me was too crude for current company, he kept it to himself—along with the fact that he'd not just been in a meaningful relationship, but married.

Chelsea had cheated on him with one of his SEAL brothers. The scandal had rocked his entire team to the core. Brothers didn't pull that shit.

It just wasn't done. *Ever.*

Morale got so bad that rather than re-up at the end of his current enlistment, Doug left the Navy. Last Wayne had heard, Doug and Chelsea moved to Oregon where they ran a coffeehouse/gym. Good riddance.

Wayne paid for the items, helped Paisley into the truck, then headed for the second portion of their date. "What's your favorite fast food?"

"Oh no. Don't think you're getting out of answering my question."

He veered into traffic. "You never specifically asked anything. But I did. What do you want for dinner? We're having a picnic, so nothing too crazy."

"If we're having a picnic, we need fried chicken."

"Done."

He turned on the radio, hoping to change topics.

A country love song didn't do much in the way of taking his mind off women.

"You know one of these days I will get it out of you?"

"I don't have a clue what you're talking about." He winked before making a right into the drive-through for Mr. Cluck.

"Whatever." She'd kicked off her sandals. Her poor feet were more swollen than that time he'd had trench foot tracking an unsavory dictator through the Amazon basin.

Once chicken and all the fixings sat between them, he drove to Los Peñasquitos Canyon Preserve, parking near the El Cuervo adobe.

"I love this place," she said, "but I'm not in the right gear or condition for a hike."

"No worries. I figure we'll take our dinner and head for that bench." He pointed to a wooden bench not far from the vehicle, but in full sight of the park's rugged beauty.

Walking side by side, she asked, "Of all of the places in San Diego we could have gone, why did you choose here?"

"It makes me feel closest to my family ranch. Whenever I've got something on my mind, this is my favorite spot to come think."

"Being a SEAL, I would've pegged you for a beach guy?"

He shrugged. "When you're on the water as much as I am, I can take it or leave it. I miss the land. It grounds me—well, not just because I'm on dirt, but—"

"I get it. It makes you feel closer to your family."

"Yeah." They'd reached the bench. He assembled a paper plate for her—chicken, slaw and rolls. Handing her a plastic fork and napkin, he added, "Despite our predicament, I'm excited for you to see my folks again. They like you."

"I like them." She bit into a drumstick and chewed. "Sorry Monica got them involved in her and Logan's wedding extravaganza."

He waved off her concern. "On some level, it's a good thing. When we last talked, it seemed to have taken Dad's mind from his situation."

"That's great. I love a silver lining."

"I can't thank you enough for going along with this. You are beyond a trooper."

"Anyone would help. It's the right thing to do."

Not anyone. Chelsea couldn't even be bothered to

offer to refill his coffee when she was already grabbing one for herself.

"What's with that dark look?" She wiped her hands, then reached out, tracing his furrowed brow. They'd been friends for a while. Her touch shouldn't have come as a shock. But it did. Even more shocking? He wouldn't have minded drawing her onto his lap for a hug. Given his history—not cool.

"Look…" He sighed, dropping his chicken breast to his plate. "I wasn't going to say anything, because it's irrelevant and frankly embarrassing, but in my early twenties, I was married."

"I knew I was onto something back in the boot store. What happened? You strike me as a forever kind of guy."

"I am—was. Thank you for saying so." He forced a few deep, calming breaths. Appreciated the rich smell of sunbaked stone, rocks and dirt. Over ten years later, Chelsea still held dark power over him. He hated that fact almost as much as he wished he hated her. But he didn't. A part of him would always love her, which hurt even more. "Long story, short? She not only cheated on me, but with a fellow SEAL. Doug. It was a seriously tough time."

"My gosh." She covered her mouth with her napkin. "That's awful."

"It was a while ago." A light breeze fluttered Paisley's hair. He fought the urge to smooth it back from her eyes. What about her did he find so intriguing? Obviously, for jumping in to help him, she had a huge heart. But there was also an indefinable something more drawing him closer. "I'm over it."

"Are you?" She finished her slaw. "Not to get personal, but in all the times I've seen you and your team partying at the pool, you've always kept to yourself. Now that I think about it, I've never even seen you frolicking with one of those bikini models."

"Never saw the need. My ex—Chelsea—ruined me for all future relationships. She taught me that giving your heart to someone is dangerous."

"When you're out on missions, don't you trust your teammates?"

"That's different."

"Not at all. Just like Doug was a bad seed amongst your team, maybe Chelsea was amongst women. Like Dr. Dirtbag was horrible to me. But just because all of them were rotten, that doesn't mean we're both doomed to a lifetime of loneliness and despair. I'd hate for my son to be raised without a father." She fingered her dress's hem. "Don't get me wrong, I'm in no hurry to throw myself into a new relationship, but someday, with the right guy, I think it would be wonderful to be loved the way I feel like I have the capacity to love."

"That's beautiful," he said. "For real. I wish I felt the same. But something inside me..." He patted his chest. "It feels broken. I honestly don't think I'll ever love again."

"That's sad. But I understand. I even respect the fact that you know yourself well enough to make that determination before hurting someone else."

In the setting sun, he took her hand, gliding on the

engagement ring he'd bought on the way to her apartment and hidden in his pocket. "I don't deserve you. But thanks again. Dad's disease scares me worse than any battle I've faced. Regardless of what happens, I want you to have this gift as my way of saying thanks."

"Wayne…" Tears pooled in her gaze as she looked from him to the sparkling diamond solitaire. "This isn't necessary. I told you I don't expect anything in return for helping."

He wanted to kiss her. It was the only logical way he could think of to get her to stop yammering about things that didn't matter. But right there, in that moment, he couldn't quite summon the nerve. Instead, he landed a perfectly harmless peck to her cheek. Only it wasn't—all that harmless—when leaning close made him notice the floral scent of her hair. He wanted to tug the ponytail holder free. See her copper waves long and wild. Most of all, he wanted his lips pressed to hers. His tongue sweeping hers. He wanted a helluva lot he had no right to be wanting.

"Anyway…" He cleared his throat, then grinned. "More than you know, I appreciate your help. Thank you."

"But—"

He forced himself back before he went and did something stupid like pressing his lips to hers. "All you have to say is 'you're welcome.'"

She raised her fingers to her lips. Was it possible she had the same inappropriate cravings? If so, didn't that make those cravings wholly *appropriate*? "But, Wayne—"

"But, Paise." Shit. *Do I have to imagine kissing you quiet all night long?*

She looked dazed—kind of like he felt. They were friends. What had he been thinking wanting to kiss her? Why did he crave even more?

"Well?" he prompted.

After a breathy giggle, she said, "You're welcome."

"Perfect."

"We're in this together now," she said, admiring her ring. "Chelsea might have left you, but I won't. Leaving a friend when they need me most has never been my style."

And that's what makes you dangerous. You're exactly the kind of woman I'd always wanted to marry...

Chapter Six

"Thanks again for my ring and hat and boots and, in general, an awesome night. I still need a wedding dress, but we have time to find one." While Wayne set her gifts on the kitchen table, Paisley covered her yawn. "Really—I can't remember the last time I had more fun."

"My pleasure." He tipped his cowboy hat. Must her pretend fiancé be so charming? The fact that he'd opened up to her only made him that much more attractive. Was it baby hormones making her swoony over her neighbor or could she be developing real feelings? The latter would be a disaster! When—*if*—she was ready for another try at romance, she couldn't pick a worse candidate than a man so opposed to marriage that he was borrowing a pregnant woman to be his pretend wife.

"I'm tired—" she gravitated toward the fridge "—but not sleepy. Does that make sense?"

"Sure. Happens to me all the time."

"Wanna make popcorn and watch a movie?"

"Depends... I don't do cartoons or chick flicks.

Oh—and musicals." He shuddered. "Those are the worst."

"Whatever. Could you please get my popper down? I usually stand on a chair, but…" She hugged her baby bump.

"Got it."

The kitchen was cramped enough with one person, but with Wayne helping to reach oil and bowls, he also ignited sparks of achy awareness and longing for an activity that had nothing to do with popcorn, but plenty with sizzle and heat.

By the time they each sat on opposite ends of the couch with snacks and apple juice—pregnant lady champagne—and Paisley started the movie, her lips curved into a secret smile.

"I need a beer." He grabbed a cold one out of the fridge. It had been stashed way in the back since before she'd found out she was pregnant. "Hey, what's got you grinning?"

"Oh, I'd love a beer." She rubbed her baby. "Sadly, this guy's underage. I was grinning because I was just thinking about how funny it is that we're about to embark on our pretend marriage, but we're already acting like an old married couple."

He rolled his eyes before catching his first glimpse of the screen. "*Jerry Maguire?* Are you kidding me? No. You knew my rules, and—"

"Give it a chance. If you're not hooked in ten minutes, we'll watch something else."

"I know I'll hate it."

"Ten minutes."

"Okay… But only because you seduced me with seriously great popcorn."

Two hours later, credits rolled.

Paisley had stretched out, landing her feet on Wayne's lap. "Are someone's eyes teary?"

"No. No way." He turned his head to wipe them. "Allergies."

"Uh-huh. It's not a crime to feel."

"It kinda is. Because every time I see a romance that works, I feel worse about mine failing."

"Stop. You were the wronged party. All you were guilty of is loving someone who turned out to be a loser."

He nodded. "How'd you get so wise?"

"*Seriously?*" She pointed at her baby. "Walking wounded here. Not only did I get cheated on, but I've got a lifelong reminder—not that I don't already love this little guy like crazy, but you know what I mean."

"Yeah. Guess we've both had our hearts put through an emotional meat grinder."

Wincing, Paisley said, "Not the most poetic of images, yet apropos."

"Know what occurred to me?"

"No clue?" She followed a sleepy yawn with a grin.

"At some point over the weekend at the ranch, we're going to have to kiss. Might be less awkward if we practice."

"I'll bet you use that line on all the ladies."

"That did sound awful. Sorry I said anything."

"I'm teasing. You're right. If we show up having

zero physical connection, your parents won't be fooled for a minute."

Rubbing his jaw, he said, "We should keep this clinical. I don't want you feeling uncomfortable."

"Thank you. Good to know my future husband is as thoughtful as he is cute."

"You think I'm *cute*?" He made a sour face. "Please don't say that around Logan. I'd never live it down."

"Promise. Mum's the word. So how do you want to work this? Logistically, I mean. It's not exactly like we can get close without special maneuvers."

"Let's see…" Grabbing her ankles, he swung her legs off his lap, then scooted closer so they sat side by side. He tried leaning in for a kiss, but couldn't get past her cheek. "I'm going to have to try a different technique." He slid off the sofa and onto his knees. Leaning forward, his face close enough for her to feel his warm exhalations on her upper lip, he asked, "Sure this is okay?"

"Uh-huh…" Though judging by her runaway pulse—nothing about this was remotely okay. More in the realm of sublime. In that instant, her body blurred the line between real and make-believe. What if Wayne was her baby's real father? How much different— better—would her life now be?

He leaned closer.

Closer.

When he finally landed his lips atop hers, kissing her with leisurely perfection, a punch-drunk giddiness flowed through her.

He drew back. "Was that all right?"

Licking her lips, she nodded. "Maybe we should amp it up—you know, just to make it extra believable."

"Got it. Good call." This time, he increased the pressure, urging her lips apart before slipping his tongue in her mouth. On a cellular level, her entire body felt lifted by excitement and hope and the prospect of this dazzling surprise she'd never seen coming. He kissed her and kissed her until she was groaning and he'd slipped to the floor, tugging her along for the ride.

Her dress rode up, baring her thighs.

But then the baby kicked, jarring her to her senses. What was she doing?

"Whoa!" Wayne shifted, helping her off his lap and straightening her dress. "Even I felt that kick. Your little guy's going to be a bruiser."

"Yeah…" Paisley struggled with her hair, her dress, her runaway pulse. What happened? For a kiss that was merely for practice, it had packed an awfully supercharged punch.

"Um…" He cleared his throat. "I should probably get going. I've got to be back on base at a hellish hour."

"I understand. Go."

"You sure?"

She nodded.

"Let's at least get you off the floor." He stood in front of her, then straddled her legs, slipping his hands beneath her arms to heft her onto the sofa. "There you go. Anything you need?"

Some semblance of pride?

Had he not been rocked to the core by that kiss? He was her friend, so why did she feel a thousand times more turned on than she ever had by Dr. Dirtbag? Or any other man?

"Paise? Needs?"

Plenty. But none readily available at the corner store.

She shook her head. "Thanks, though."

He nodded. "Okay, well…catch you later." His half wave and forced smile made her cringe.

As soon as he left, she drowned her frustration in a freezer-burned pint of cookie dough ice cream.

WHAT HAVE I DONE?

Wayne tightened his grip on the truck's wheel, still five hours out from his parents' ranch, driving across a sea of sand with a sky so clear and blue he could see all the way to heaven. What the hell was he doing in the Navy when his soul belonged on this land?

Paisley slept hugging the pregnancy pillow he'd bought her, resting her head against the window. She'd turned her back to him.

The night they'd picnicked and practiced kissing had been hands down one of the nicest in recent memory. He hadn't wanted it to end. He'd envisioned the two of them doing way more than kissing, sharing the warmth of Paisley's bed, spooning the swell of her belly even after she'd fallen into a deep sleep.

He'd wanted to send flowers to her office, but his CO had been crankier than usual, meaning Wayne hadn't had a chance to make the call. The only thing she'd ever asked of him was to keep in touch, yet he hadn't even managed shooting her a single text.

Not cool.

The rest of the week had brought the same—erratic work hours dictated he was literally underwater while everyone else slept.

But it wasn't everyone else he was worried about. He wondered what Paisley was thinking. Was she pissed by the way he'd left? Did she think he hadn't cared? She was a good friend. The last thing he wanted was for her to think he was taking unfair advantage of her offer to pose as his fiancée.

In the same breath, he wished he could stop thinking about her. He wasn't sure what he felt—if it could even be labeled. All he knew was that he cared a little too much for a woman intended to be his pretend wife.

The night before their trip, he hit a twenty-four-hour warehouse store to pick up essentials. Her favorite snacks of gummy bears and jerky, along with apple juice boxes and animal crackers and Sprite. He'd grabbed her a special pregnancy pillow and even mellow mood music the clerk had assured him would soothe his *wife*.

How awful was he to not correct the woman?

In that moment, he'd have given anything to have met Paisley before Chelsea. If he'd made vows to her, might everything now be different? Might her baby be his?

That morning, when he'd taken her bags, stowing them in the truck bed, she'd thanked him, but hadn't made eye contact. Understandably, she was pissed. He didn't blame her. But in his defense, she'd known the score.

You're an ass.

Absolutely. But that fact couldn't change his past. It couldn't make him any less determined to remain single for the rest of his life.

PAISLEY WOKE WITH drool on her chin and a stiff neck.

Eyes fully open, she found herself still in Wayne's truck, flying through a foreign landscape void of anything save for distant mountains and the occasional cactus, rocks and sand.

"How much longer?" she asked.

"Couple hours. You okay?"

"I wouldn't turn down a bathroom, but I don't see a 7-Eleven."

"There's a truck stop about thirty miles from here. Can you make it till then?"

"Do I have a choice?" She turned down the volume on the stereo. "What's this crazy music? It sounds like whales mating with dolphins."

"It's supposed to be soothing for you and the baby. The salesclerk says it simulates being in the womb."

"Hmm." Lips pursed, she turned back to the barren view. "Good thing the clerk knows what's going on in there—in my womb."

"I tried sending you flowers."

"Why?" He'd been up-front with her from the start that their initial kiss had been for practice. About putting on a good show for his parents. She had no right to be hurt about his not so much as calling to say hello since. But she *was* hurt.

Deeply.

She swallowed the knot at the back of her throat.

"I wanted to send flowers," he said, "because it would have been a nice gesture. You deserved them."

"For being a good kisser?"

"More like being an overall great human."

He turned off the pan flutes and gentle waves and lonely whales. "Is it my imagination, or am I sensing a boatload of hostility?"

"No." She looked at him, but then turned away, hugging her pillow. "Maybe. Honestly? I'd be lying if I said I wasn't crushed when you bolted from my apartment as if the place was on fire. When a week passes and you didn't call or even stop by after work?" She sharply exhaled. "Yeah, I was pissed. But I shouldn't have been. We're neighbors—nothing more. Only now, we're neighbors who've shared a few kisses who also happen to have a pretend engagement."

"I get why you're mad. But please understand my commanding officer wouldn't care if I was making out with a Kardashian. When I'm on duty, I'm on duty. Period. He's had us working beach insertion drills during ungodly hours. I had to buy your pillow and snacks at four in the morning."

"One Kardashian in particular? Or all of them?" The bad joke was Paisley's stab at deflecting. She had been devastated by his not calling or stopping by. But she shouldn't have been. According to the parameters of their sham-engagement that she'd helped establish, the whole point was to keep it casual. Simple. No harm, no foul. All of which had been no big deal till she'd kissed him. And kissed him.

Now, she was all messed up inside.

She found herself no longer wanting to be his friend, but to take his hand. Or maybe stroke her finger up his tanned forearm, testing to see if the coarse hairs glinting in the sun really had been spun from gold.

But why do any of those things when, technically, she wasn't into Wayne, right? Dr. Dirtbag ruined her, right? She owed it to her baby to focus on her career and motherhood. Who even had time for a guy, *right*?

"I know what happened the other night was wrong." Wayne adjusted the air vent, directing it her way. "Too warm? You look flushed."

"I'm fine."

"Good. Don't need you passing out on me. Do you feel properly hydrated? It gets hot out here."

"We're in an air-conditioned truck—not a covered wagon."

"What's got you so salty?"

You! Your stupid chiseled perfection. Your sexy grin. The way your eyes turn shark-fin gray when you're talking about serious subjects, but have a silvery glow when you smile.

Taking a deep breath, she forced a serene expression. "I'm good. Sleepy, but good."

"How are your ankles?"

"Fine. Why?"

"I bought *What to Expect When You're Expecting* for the Kindle app on my phone. Turns out lots of pregnant ladies get swollen ankles when traveling. *Cankles*, for short. When we hit the truck stop, you should walk around a little—just to keep your blood flowing."

"Tell you what." She shifted the pillow, trying and

failing to get comfortable. "I'll walk if you promise not to talk."

"Considering you're going to see your future in-laws soon, that's not a very nice attitude." He winked, but she wasn't in the mood for playing.

She was tired.

She hadn't yet given birth, but already she feared the added stress of being a single mom. If she was brutally honest with herself, maybe the reason she was upset with Wayne had nothing to do with him, but everything with her.

For an instant, with him holding her, kissing her, making her feel cherished if only for that short while, she'd dared fantasize about them marrying for real. Now, in the too harsh light of day, she realized that was never going to happen.

But maybe I secretly want it to happen?

Not with Wayne per se, but someone. The thought of being alone the rest of her life brought on the kind of soul-crushing pain that usually left her reaching for an entire pot of holistic antacid.

Miles later, by the time Wayne pulled his truck alongside a gas pump, Paisley wasn't sure whether her bladder or pride hurt worse.

Wayne opened her door for her, offering his hand to help soften her landing on the sun-cracked concrete, but she held up her hands. "Thanks. I can manage."

Sure, you can. Gravity provided more than adequate assistance on the way down, but who was going to help her get back in? She glanced over her shoulder to find Wayne still staring.

With everything in her, she wanted to glare, but forced a half smile. What was wrong with her? Why couldn't she just as easily force herself to get over what they'd shared? It had been a few kisses between friends. No big deal. Even his explanation for walking out made perfect sense.

The only thing that didn't was the way she was over-reacting.

The walk inside took far too long, dodging SUVs and minivans. The only civilization for miles was as hot, windy and dusty as it was crowded. It seemed every family on the road for the long holiday weekend must be using this highway.

After waiting her turn in the restroom, Paisley wandered down aisle after aisle loaded with everything, including groceries, clothing, and souvenirs when she eyed a trinket that made her smile.

On a whim, she took it to an out-of-view side register.

The zigzagging return trek across the treacherous lot was made even more hazardous when Wayne darted out from behind her, grabbing hold of her elbow as if she were ninety-year-old granny with a walker— although, at the moment, the stability of a walker might come in handy. Could those things be outfitted with a cup holder?

He said, "You can't stay mad at me forever."

True. But she could at least until they reached his parents' ranch.

"You said yourself you don't even have anything to be mad about."

There was nothing Paisley despised more than a man who threw her own logic back in her face.

When they finally reached the truck, Wayne opened the passenger-side door, essentially forcing her to grab hold of the seat back with one hand and him with the other. Entering his truck was always an awkward affair, but this time, with her added gear in the way, she might as well have been boarding the space shuttle. She landed with enough force to drag Wayne partially down with her, landing with a soft thump of pillow and leather and masculine-smelling body parts she fought not to recognize.

"Oh—hey. Didn't mean for that to get strange." He backed away before further humiliating her by manhandling her into a proper seating position, brushing the backs of his hands across her full, ridiculously sensitive breasts to fasten her seat belt, then closing her door.

Once he sat back behind the wheel, he fished something from his jeans pocket. "While I was inside, I saw this—reminded me of our cornball trip to the fake wedding cake store."

"You've got to be kidding."

"What…" He looked crestfallen. "It's corny, but kinda cute—in a cheese-ball way."

She reached in her pocket, pulling out the identical Christmas ornament that looked like a miniature version of Wayne's favorite "fake cake." The one with the miniature cacti and the cowboy hat topper.

How could she stay mad at a guy who had chosen— from all of the thousands of items in that store ranging from rattlesnake salt-and-pepper shakers to windshield wiper replacement blades—the same goofy souvenir as her?

They both burst out laughing, exchanging gifts and then rushed apologies.

"I'm sorry," she blurted.

"No, I really am sorry. That night was…" He sharply exhaled. "Let's just say that if we were married?" He met her gaze, fixing her with a stare that left her incapable of finding air. "Well, if I were your man for real… I'd be a helluva lucky guy."

Her cheeks burned like a super volcano—not that she was complaining. Even the baby was in danger of swooning!

Ducking her gaze, she licked her lips. "I—I feel the same. Maybe once we get to the ranch, we might—"

HONK! Honk, honk, hooooooonk!

They both glanced through the rear window to find the guy driving the RV behind them red faced for an entirely different reason. "Keep it moving, buddy! I don't have all day!"

Wayne grinned. "Hold that thought—yours, Paise. For sure, not his."

The rest of the trip passed in a blur.

They ditched the whale song in favor of '90s emo, which Paisley found more than a little shocking. "You do know you're killing your cowboy rep?"

"I'll take the hit. He clutched his chest. "Taking Back Sunday feels my pain."

She wished she could say the closer they got to Wayne's own slice of heaven, the better she felt, but truthfully, her stomach worked overtime with more indigestion. The thought of seeing Wayne's dying father literally made her sick.

How would she shake his hand without falling apart?

And what would she do about Wayne's poor mom, who would soon be a widow? To think she and Wayne had been bickering had been a ridiculous waste of precious time. It made Paisley feel ashamed to have lost sight of their primary goal—to help ease his father's emotional pain.

"Prepare me for what to expect," she asked. "Is your dad in a wheelchair? Does he spend most of his time in bed?"

"He can't—at least not without my mom knowing the full score. I've repeatedly asked for details, but Dad's deliberately keeping me in the dark. Says he doesn't want to bother me."

"Let's just keep our expectations open," Paisley said. "That way, if he spends most of his time in, say, a recliner or on the couch, you'll be pleasantly surprised."

"That's a positive way of looking at it." He tightened his grip on the wheel. "Then there's Mom. While I'm here. I need to have a hard talk with her. I'm not sure she's capable of caring for the ranch on her own, and I've got almost seventeen months left on my current enlistment before I could even think about getting out here to help."

"Is that something you see yourself doing? Retiring from the navy to live here?"

He released a troubled sigh. "I always planned on putting in my twenty years before leaving the military, but now? I'm not sure. I love what I do. But there's something about being on the back of a horse first thing in the morning. There's a fine mist rising off the land, and for miles in every direction there's not a soul around, not a creature stirring save for maybe an eagle soaring far above your head. You get this gut-deep feeling of truth. As if you're one with the earth. It's profound." He swiped tears with the backs of his hands. "Lord… This whole thing with my dad is getting to me. I sound nuttier than a peanut butter cookie."

"Not really. If anything, you made me want to share your experience. Arizona should pay you to be a travel spokesperson."

"Sounds about right. Funny how when you're a stupid kid, you fight so damned hard to get away from a place, then once you grow up, all you want to do is get back."

"Hmm…" She rubbed her baby bump.

"How about you? Anyplace special in your past?"

"Nope." Was now the right time to confide in him about her rocky history? Or never? It wasn't as if they'd be together long-term. The fewer people who knew about her mother, the better.

Wayne cleared his throat. "A while back, at one of your pool parties—that one when Monica bought you the car you didn't accept?"

"Yes?" Why did she have the feeling she wouldn't like what he was about to say next?"

"She mentioned a bit about your mom I'm guessing you wouldn't have appreciated getting out. She'd had a fair amount to drink—you know Monica when she doesn't get what she sets her sights on… Anyway, if you ever want to talk about it, seeing how I've got my own fair share of ghosts haunting my closet, I'm here."

"Thanks."

Just how much did he know?

She'd be mortified if he discovered her mother's full story. The worst of it was thankfully over, but the shame remained. No matter how much Paisley distanced herself from her past, she somehow always ended up feeling as if she were right back on the wrong side of the tracks. All she'd ever wanted was to feel respectable. To feel part of a real family. Part of something bigger than herself. As if she finally belonged.

Was that too much to ask?

Apparently so.

Hugging her baby, she swallowed the knot in her throat.

"What's got you so deep in thought?" Wayne asked.

"The weather."

"Humph." His narrowed-eyed stare called her out. "That's what I thought."

Chapter Seven

Driving the last few miles down the ranch's winding dirt road might as well have been Christmas as opposed to almost Easter. That was how exited Wayne felt by the prospect of once again seeing his parents and this wondrous place.

Towering copper-toned rock formations set the backdrop for emerald pastures nourishing some of the finest breeding cattle in the country. Crayola couldn't invent a sky color more perfectly, dazzlingly blue.

He rolled down the windows to get his first taste of the smell—to others, that might seem like an odd way to describe the scent of a place, but that's the way it made him feel. That's how potent it was. As if he could taste *and* smell the ponderosa pine and grass and soil and clean air all at once.

"Wayne, roll up your window! You're wrecking my hair, and your mom's going to think I'm a savage." Paisley cupped her hands to her head.

"What are you talking about?" By way of compromise, he rolled up her window. "We went through a damned sandstorm back at the truck stop."

"That was different. I could control which direction my hair was flowing."

"Please, hush. You're running the moment."

"The moment? Hate to burst your bubble there, cowboy, but we've been on a tooth-rattling dirt road for— *Oh my…*"

"Told you." He glanced her way, beaming with pride. "Behold. Rio Bravo Ranch." He added in a teasing tone, "In case I failed to mention it, my dad has a thing for John Wayne."

"That's adorable."

"Not so much when you lived with him." Wayne laughed.

"You said it was a house, but this is a hacienda. Look at all the arches and the tile roof. It's so romantic. I see why Monica wanted her wedding here."

Wayne laughed. "No kidding, right? I can't blame her."

His father had the place custom built over decades, paying as he went along. The bedrooms, kitchen and living areas all wound around a center courtyard that, besides ranching, had been his dad's life passion. The summer garden with its center three-tier fountain was spectacular.

"I can't wait to explore."

"I can't wait to guide you."

He enjoyed her smile a little too much.

Wait—was that even a thing?

Rounding the bend that would give Paisley her first view of the hundred-year-old barn Wayne and his parents lived in before building the house, he caught himself momentarily holding his breath. He couldn't wait for her reaction to not just the impressive historic structure, but the majestic panoramic view of what felt like the entire Prescott National Forest. "Well? What do you think?"

Having seen the view himself, just this once, he looked to her, and was beyond disappointed.

"I'm horrified. Wayne, I'm so sorry."

"What do you—" He turned to look in the direction she was staring. *Are you kidding me?* The normally postcard-perfect view of big skies and grazing horses and far-off, snowcapped mountains had been defiled by a half-dozen trucks with Boutique Bridal written in giant hot pink script across the sides. Around those trucks were delivery vans and a whipped-up hornet's nest of frenzied workers. "Is all of this Monica's doing?"

"Probably a safe bet. But please don't be too hard on her."

He coughed to keep from releasing a string of expletives. "Can you imagine what the stress of this is doing to my poor parents?"

She winced. "On the bright side, maybe it's taken their minds off the inevitable?"

"You're not helping."

"Relax. Forget about Monica and Logan's Godzilla-sized wedding and let's focus on having a successful first meeting as a couple with your mom and dad. We probably should at the very first hold hands. Maybe even throw in a little canoodling."

"What's that?" he asked while driving his truck

around to the side of the house where his dad had positioned the garage so as not to mar the front facade.

"Canoodling? I'm not sure of the actual definition. It's like when couples aren't really all over each other per se, but kinda cuddly. Like you might spontaneously kiss my cheek. And I might rub your shoulder or chest."

"Interesting."

"We don't have to. But it might add a more realistic touch to what's starting to feel like a sinking ship."

"Toss in more of what happened the other night, and I think I like canoodling." He grinned before parking the truck, turning off the engine, then climbing out. "Hang tight. In case Mom's on her way outside, you should let me help you."

"Agreed."

Just as his mother burst out the home's side door, Wayne opened Paisley's door for her to slide into his waiting arms. Their timing was perfect. But nothing beat the all-too-pleasurable sensation of holding Paisley again.

"Wayne! You're finally here. And Paisley! Welcome to the family, honey. Peter and I couldn't be more thrilled to have you."

"Thank you, Mrs. Brustanovitch."

"Pease, call me Jules. And let me see that gorgeous engagement ring."

Wayne would be first to admit feeling like a jackass for duping his mom—especially when he'd never seen her happier. Hugging Paisley raised a glow to her cheeks and sparkle to her blue eyes like he hadn't seen since introducing her to Chelsea, yet look how that turned out. "Where's Dad?"

"He's coming. You know your father. He's got himself knee-deep in all the festivities. Last I saw he was making sure no one upset Bruce."

"Who's Bruce?" Paisley asked. Per the canoodling plan, she took his hand, resting her head against his shoulder. He, in turn, wrapped his arm around her shoulders, giving her a light, reassuring squeeze. Yes, this was good. Maybe a little too good, judging by cravings to practice honeymoon techniques.

"Peter's prized bull. I swear that animal gets more attention than the rest of us combined."

"While Dad's not here..." Wayne bowed his head, unsure how to broach the elephant in the room of his father's disease. "How's he doing?"

"Fine. Not that he'd ever let you know it, but on chilly mornings his arthritis bothers him. I tell him to spend a little less time in the saddle and more time golfing with his buddies, but he refuses to listen."

Wayne and Paisley shared a look.

"Guess if that's all he has to complain about, that's good."

"Come on in. Paisley, I'm sure you're exhausted from that drive, so I've got your room ready. Wayne, you're bunking in your old room. No funny business before the wedding." His mother wagged her finger, then winked.

Once Wayne's mom had Paisley settled in a guest room with a stunning view of Mount Rockwell, promising to return with fresh-baked cookies, he made quick work of retrieving all the luggage.

Finished, he found Paisley stretched across the bed looking her usual adorably mussed self while reading a magazine with her swollen feet up on a pillow.

"Did you catch that?" He closed the door.

"About your dad?" She tossed her magazine aside to sit up—or, at least, try. He perched on the bed beside her. "I looked for him, and he's nowhere in that crowd. Where would he go? Last time we talked, he said he was practically on life support."

"None of this makes sense."

"Tell me about it."

"Want to go look for him together?"

He pointed to her feet. "According to the expectant mother guide I read, you shouldn't be going anywhere with those swollen ankles. What's the technical term again? *Cankles*?"

"I'm fine," she said with a near growl. "Help me up. Besides, I want to visit with your mom and see the rest of the house and grounds before dark."

He stood, then held out his hand. "When do Monica and Logan get in?"

"First thing in the morning. Monica's dad's flying most of her family in to a local airstrip. Clip's?"

"Clem's—named after his daughter, Clementine. We dated in tenth grade."

"Should I be jealous?"

"Absolutely. That girl could calf rope like nobody's business. I always did mean to date a rodeo queen. She won a few crowns the summer before our senior year. Maybe I should look her up while I'm in town?"

"Stop." She elbowed him. "You're almost a pretend married man."

"Relax." He winked. "Last I heard, I'm pretty sure she's a for-real married woman with three kids and a one-eyed dog named Peanut. I know because she also happens to be the woman who keeps my mom perpetually blonde."

"You're awful." On their way out of the room, Paisley elbowed him again. Oddly enough, Wayne didn't mind. He kind of liked teasing her. She made him—if for only a few minutes—forget the harsh reality he faced in accepting the serious nature of his dad's condition.

That said, as he took her hand, guiding her through the single-level home's maze of rooms to the kitchen, Wayne had to remind himself that none of this was real. No matter how warm and fuzzy being with Paisley made him feel, that didn't change the fact that he'd thought he'd been in love once before and he'd been wrong.

Moral of the story? There was no such thing as lasting love. Sure—maybe in rare cases like with his folks, but even they were doomed to have their hearts broken.

With his dad gone, his poor mom may never recover.

He owed it to his mother to shield his own heart. To stay strong.

On their way through the living room, Paisley paused, taking in the same view that had gotten him through multiple tours in Iraq. Sunlight kissed her coppery hair, making a few strands look as lucky and shiny as a new penny. One of his favorite things about her was that she had no idea just how lovely she really was.

In another time, he could have totally seen himself with her. Now it was too late for them both. They'd been through too much to ever wipe their emotional slates clean. On their picnic, Paisley had said she was all for giving love another shot, but for the life of him, he didn't understand why. As her friend, he'd even go so far as to say he felt honor bound to dissuade her.

"When our engagement is done," he asked, "do you think you'll date?"

"Probably not right away. The baby will need all of my attention for a while."

"I'll help."

"With the baby?" Her eyes widened as if he'd suggested assisting her with her next decorating project.

"Would that be so awful? You mentioned wanting a father in his life. Well—I can't be that, but I could make a great father figure. We'll play catch. I'll take him fishing. That kind of stuff."

She grinned. "You do know he's not popping out of the womb ready for bro dates?"

"You know what I mean. All I'm saying is that I'm not going anywhere. You made that promise to me and I'm repaying the favor. I'll help with other stuff, too. Diapers. Baths. Babysitting if you need to run to the store. Whatever."

"Thanks. I appreciate the offer." Her smile seemed different. Easier. More relaxed. He liked it. In the future, he'd enjoy seeing more of the same.

"You're welcome." Wayne realized he still held her hand. He should have let go, but he hadn't.

"I thought I heard voices." Wayne's mom entered the room. "Paisley, hon, I thought you were napping."

"I tried, but somebody—" she elbowed Wayne "—is so excited for me to get reacquainted with his dad and see the rest of your gorgeous house and land that he woke me. I'm supposed to be getting a tour, but this is as far as we've gotten."

"This has always been one of my favorite rooms. Peter got the beams for the ceiling from a local forest after a fire. Once he scraped down the charred outer layers, underneath was such beauty." Wayne watched Paisley looking at the stucco-and-beamed ceiling. He and his dad had spent weeks high on a ladder, hand-oiling the beams till they shone. The thought of his looming death was inconceivable.

It was— A sob escaped him.

"Sweetie?" his mom asked.

"Babe?" Paisley rubbed his back, her voice laced with concern.

"I'm good," he said. "It's just a lot. I don't know how you're keeping it together."

"Keeping what together? Hon, I don't know—"

"There my big, strapping hunk of American boy! Look how you grow! Come here to Papa." For his and Paisley's benefit, Wayne assumed his dad must be forcing his good cheer. Wayne went to him, crushing him in a hug. He'd missed everything about him from his thick Russian accent to his rich pipe tobacco smell. "It so good to see you. And you—" He released his son to turn his attention to Paisley. "Let me have a feel of my grandson. You name him John Wayne Jr., no?"

"Um, no? Yes? I'm not really sure?" Laughing, Paisley held out her hand for him to shake. "Either way, it's nice seeing you again."

"No handshake with family. You my daughter. Hug only." Wayne fought back fresh tears at the sight of his dad and Paisley's warm embrace. She was amazing for doing this for him. Now that he had a closer look at his father, he noticed that his complexion did seem unnaturally pale. In his condition, Wayne supposed it was to be expected. "Come, let us eat. Your momma made delicious stew. My Wayne's favorite. We eat fancy food with strangers tomorrow. But tonight, for family. Tonight, we celebrate our new daughter and baby cowboy!"

PAISLEY WASN'T SURE what she'd expected from her initial reaction to Wayne's family ranch or spending quality time with his actual family, but as she sat at the rough-hewn pine kitchen table, watching them all flow through dinner cleanup with the ease of people who've lived and loved together for years, an old familiar pang hurt deep inside her.

This is what she'd wanted for herself and Dr. Dirtbag and their child. The kind of belonging that no amount of money could buy. The only price was love. Her mother had sadly never learned that lesson.

Peter was utterly charming, and putting on such a brave front. His complexion wasn't right. A pasty gray. When even Jules commented he didn't look well, he'd told her that as soon as his grandson was born, he would feel like a new man. Judging by his big smile, he meant it, which put even more pressure on Paisley to deliver a stellar performance.

At the same time, watching this tight unit of three wash dishes and wipe down counters, a small voice inside played devil's advocate. What happened if Wayne got the miracle he'd been seeking and Peter did survive?

At what point did she and Wayne come clean?

When she'd first arrived on their ranch carrying the lie, she'd considered it a mercy mission. Now she wasn't so sure. The thought of these kindhearted people opening their home and lives to her when she was a fraud was mortifying. It made her feel as if at her core, she was no better than her mom. It didn't matter that this lie had been intended to help Peter.

A lie was a lie.

At what point in this process had she forgotten that fact?

Jules and Peter were such easy people to love.

And Wayne…

Paisley ducked her flaming cheeks by sipping the herbal tea Jules delivered. "Wayne said you had a rough time of it your first couple trimesters?"

"The worst. Knock on wood, I seem to be much better now."

"Good." Jules joined her at the table while the men finished washing the pots and pans. In a conspiratorial tone, she said, "I can't tell you how tickled I am to see Wayne happy again. What that Chelsea put him through should be a crime. The poor boy walked around like a zombie for years. But with you… *Oh!*" She cupped her hand to Paisley's belly. "He kicked so hard I saw it! Peter! Come here! Our grandson kicked!"

"Praise be!" Peter held his hands up to the heavens. "We are a family inordinately blessed."

Paisley would have thought she'd feel awkward about Jules and Peter each edging their chairs closer to place their hands over her tummy, but she didn't mind. If anything, their affection filled her with an achy yearning she felt clear to her toes. How was it possible to have only been on the ranch mere hours, yet already feel part of this tight-knit family unit?

How lucky Wayne was.

How devastated she would feel when their charade culminated in Peter's funeral.

Peter said, "My new daughter, Paze-lee, I have idea. Wayne spend so much time doing army man, you must stay with us when baby come. My beautiful Jules, she make sure you have best of everything. I teach baby about cattle and horses and how to be best American cowboy."

Paisley glanced to Wayne. *Help!*

He nodded. "Dad, that's an amazing offer, but slow down. If and when I'm deployed, Paisley might enjoy staying here, but for now, she'll stick with me near base."

"Of course." Peter's smile faded. His shoulders hunched. "I understand."

"Stop pouting," Jules playfully scolded. "We'll have plenty of time with the baby on weekends and holidays. Of course, we'd have even more if our new little family ever wanted to move into the apartment above the barn. It's adorable, Paisley. I'm sure you'll see it. That's where Monica's staying."

Paisley raised her eyebrows. Somehow, she couldn't imagine her friend bunking in a barn. But then she'd never envisioned Monica marrying in one, either. Guess there was a first for everything.

"I've got an idea." Jules rose with an excited clap. "It's such a gorgeous night, let's eat dessert on the patio. I want to hear about how you two lovebirds transitioned from neighbors to a romantic couple. Peter, would you mind grabbing plates, forks and napkins. I'll carry the cake." She grabbed the golden-brown creation in its glass dome on her way out of the kitchen. "Paisley, for future reference, this pineapple upside down cake has always been Wayne's favorite. Don't leave without the recipe."

"I—I won't."

"How are you doing?" Wayne whispered in her ear on their way outside. His mom led the way while his father lagged with his assignment. "You seem to be handling this like a pro."

"Shouldn't you help your dad?"

"I will, but I'm concerned about you. I know this is a lot to take in. I wanted to thank you again. You'll never know how much it means to—"

Crash!

The sound of shattered glass erupted from the kitchen.

Paisley and Wayne rushed to check on his dad, only to find him on the floor.

Chapter Eight

"Dad? What happened? Are you hurt?"

"I trip," Peter said with a shrug. "Nothing serious. Unless your momma kill me for breaking dishes."

"Peter…" Jules entered the kitchen, hands on her hips. "What happened?"

"I told you rug in front of sink would kill me and look what happened." He grinned up at Wayne. "Your momma—she try kill me."

Wayne held out his hand to his father. "Let me help you up, then I'll clean this mess. You take a breather."

"I'll bring the cake inside," Paisley offered.

"No need for that," Jules said. "I appreciate the offer, but we have plenty more plates to proceed with our original plans. Only this time, I'll carry them."

"Don't you think Dad should rest?" Wayne asked.

"Why?" Jules cocked her head.

"He looks tired." As was starting to be a habit, Wayne caught himself sharing yet another look with Paisley. Call him crazy, but now he was leaning more toward the reality that his prideful father hadn't told his mom he was dying.

Was he that far into denial?

Or that hopeful he was destined for a miracle?

"His color's off, but it's barely eight o'clock. We usually don't go to bed for hours. Come on, let's get to the patio. We'll make a fire in the pit and stargaze and hear all about every detail of your whirlwind romance with Paisley."

Wayne gulped.

After the shattered glass was swept and more plates gathered and taken outside, a crackling fire was built. With the air fragrant with pinyon smoke, Jules served everyone slices of her decadent cake and then refused to be put off a moment longer.

"I've waited long enough. Tell me everything."

Wayne shared a cushioned wrought iron sofa with Paisley. She'd kicked off her sandals and now leaned against his chest. Every so often, when her storytelling grew animated, her soft hair brushed the underside of his chin. He smelled lilacs in her shampoo and remembered her kissing him with her curtain of long hair wreathing their faces.

The memory of that night was so visceral, he curved his fingers into fists. He had to physically stop himself from losing his grip on reality. This moment of enjoyment. If he took it at face value—the crickets, the stars, what might very well be the last time he bore witness to his parents' shared laughter—he was terrified of doing something stupid. Like suggesting to Paisley they double down and go all in. Make this sham engagement the real deal. But in the end, no matter how tempting the notion may be for the short term, years later, when she discovered he wasn't emotionally equipped to give her everything a husband should, she'd only resent him for ever asking.

So Wayne held himself back from stroking her hair. Or tugging it free of its ponytail holder to watch fire-light play in the copper waves.

"There we were in this bakery," Paisley said, "and I hadn't had a decent appetite in forever, so I was seriously looking forward to a yummy bite of cake. But then this crazy baker says she specializes in *fake* cakes, then she actually picks up this monstrosity of a tiered cake and tossed it at Wayne."

Wayne's mother gasped.

"I know, right?" Paisley laughed. Wayne should have been focused on his father. Catering to his every need, but now, all he could do was think about how once his father had passed, telling his mom the true nature of his relationship with Paisley would only further break her already grief-stricken heart.

"What did you do?" Jules asked, leaning forward with her elbows on her knees in rapt interest.

"I wanted to walk out," Paisley admitted. "But your son here—" she delivered a sideways jab "—went ahead and rented one. It was a ridiculous-looking thing. Great big cake with dozens of little cacti all over it instead of something more traditional—like roses. Oh—and instead of a bride and groom at the top, there was a giant cowboy hat. I suppose given the right proportions it could have been all right, but this one…" She shook her head. "What's even funnier…" She continued with the story about how they'd each picked out matching

Christmas ornaments that resembled the cake while inside the truck stop.

"I like cowboy cake." Wayne's dad slapped the thighs of his jeans from laughing. "My boy have, how you say? Good taste?"

Wayne nodded. He'd had more than enough family togetherness for one night. The gravity of what he and Paisley had done was starting to take a toll.

His parents were already falling hard for the woman they thought would in a few days be their daughter-in-law. Maybe the wisest thing for him to do at this point would be to keep them away from Paisley? No sense in them growing fonder of her when she wouldn't be a permanent fixture.

His mother howled with laughter. "Paisley, you are the breath of fresh air this house has needed. Really, you're the answer to my every prayer for our son. Isn't that right, Peter?"

"Amen," his father said with a solemn nod. Wiping tears, his father added, "You two make sentimental old man very happy. Me and baby grandson cowboy spend many happy days on this ranch."

"Now you've got me crying," Jules said with a smiling sob. "Old man, take me to bed before I make a complete fool of myself."

"Beautiful wife…" Peter stood before gracing her with a formal bow, "…nothing would make me happier." He held out his hand to her, she accepted, and off they went, giggling like a couple of teens, into the night.

For a good twenty minutes, the only sound aside

from the crackling fire, wind high in the pines and crickets was the pounding of Wayne's pulse.

He didn't like the direction his thoughts were leading, and needed to talk. As was starting to be his new normal, the only person he could trust was Paisley.

"Hear me out." Wayne cleared his throat. "I'm going to say something and, at first, you might think it's out there, but—"

"Let me guess—you don't think your dad's quite *as* sick as he let on?"

"How did you know what I was going to say?" He lurched upright to read her expression, but that left her in need of support, so he shoved a few pillows behind her back.

"Because I've been thinking it ever since the dishes were broken. Speaking from experience, that glass would have been everywhere—not in a neat little pile. It looked like he dropped them just close enough to the tile floor to make a loud noise, then lie down—far away, so he wouldn't get cut."

Wayne nodded. "I read that whole scene the same."

"A way bigger issue than that is the fact that your mom seems oblivious to him being sick."

"Yes.

"For that matter, aside from his dubious complexion, he doesn't seem remotely under the weather."

"My thoughts exactly." Wayne growled. "If I find out he faked this whole thing to manipulate me into—"

"What are you going to do? If he is faking, that's kind of wonderful, right? I mean, come on? That means your dad's not dying. And if he's not? Well, neither of us are cut out to be detectives, but we can come clean about our true situation. We did mean well. Either way, don't make any moves until after Monica and Logan's wedding. We don't want family fireworks to ruin their big day."

"Agreed." He stared into the fire. "Now what?"

"We go to bed. Start over again in the morning. Only we'll have a cast of hundreds to fool." Paisley raised her arms over her head, stretching and yawning.

Which made Wayne follow suit. "I guess I am tired. Wanna fool around first?"

"No!"

He winked. "I'm messing with you. Testing your resolve. Worth a try. Sex is a proven stress reliever."

"Uh-huh…whatever!" She tossed a throw pillow at him, but missed. "Playing devil's advocate, if your dad is sick, but his desire to spend time with his fictional future grandson is so strong that he's determined to live, what then?"

"Guess I could rent you and lil' Johnny Wayne for a weekend."

"Mister, you are just asking for trouble." She tried lunging, but lucky for him, Paisley had the dexterity of an upside-down turtle.

"Bring it on, sugar. *Double dare you.*" Had he whispered that last part? He wasn't sure how it happened, but Wayne found himself leaning over her, bracing one hand on the settee's back and the other on the armrest. Meanwhile, Paisley's plump lips were well within kissing range and getting closer all the time.

She opened them just wide enough to dart out her

tongue for a slow lick. "I, ah, thought we were headed to bed?"

"I have to tend the fire."

"Shouldn't you do that?"

Damn, but his heart was beating hard. "Thought that was what I was doing."

Because he was a damned fool when it came to anything other than official navy business, Wayne closed the distance and pressed his lips to hers, trying to physically convey the urgency his body had felt every second he'd been near her, yet not touching her, holding her and doing a whole lot of other nifty tricks he'd love to perfect.

"Mmm…" she groaned, shifting he assumed to try making room for him beside her.

He made a valiant effort to recline next to her, but ended up flat on his ass, perilously close to catching his hair on fire.

"That could have gone better." She covered her mouth to hide a smile, but there was no hiding the twinkle in her eyes.

"You laughing at me?"

"You do look awfully funny."

"Excuse me for trying to get some. It's been a long day, and if I don't have beer, I figured at least I could fill up on—"

"Sex with the desperate pregnant lady?" Shaking her head, even in the dying fire's dim light, there was no mistaking her slit-eyed look of disappointment. "See you in the morning, Wayne."

"Paise, wait." From his resting place on the patio,

he reached for her, but anger must have improved her dexterity as she was already up and waddling for the patio door. "You know I was just messing around!" he shouted after her.

The door opened and closed.

Sighing, he gazed up at the stars, clasping his hands over his forehead. What was he doing? He'd come to the ranch steeled for the reality of his father's looming death, but Paisley had somehow taken center stage. Why couldn't he keep his mind focused where it needed to be? On his dad?

After dowsing the fire, he paced beneath the stars.

When that did nothing to ease the frustration and confusion simmering in his heart, Wayne sought comfort the only place that made sense...

"WAYNE?" PAISLEY ROLLED over to find him standing alongside her bed, stripping down to his boxers. Pale moonlight made him even more beautiful, accentuating the hard planes of his shoulders and biceps and abs. "What are you doing?"

"I can't sleep. Is it okay if I crash with you?"

"No."

"Please?"

"Why?"

"My mind won't stop racing. When I'm with you..." In the dark, she heard his breath hitch. "I can't explain how, but everything feels better. Please, let me stay. Promise I won't try anything. I just need sleep."

"O-okay."

Out of her line of sight, she felt him tossing back the

sheet and quilt, and climbing in behind her. He snuggled deliciously close, spooning her, with his big hand warming her baby. "Go back to sleep. I didn't mean to wake you."

"You did." She'd be lying if she said being this close to him, with their bare limbs entwined, didn't create all manner of havoc, resulting in warm heat pooling between her legs. But she was still mad at him for apparently thinking she was *easy.*

When nothing could be further from the truth.

She could count the number of men she'd been with on one hand, and she'd loved them all.

He snuggled closer, burying his face in her hair, whispering something unintelligible before mere heartbeats later he drifted into a heavy sleep and light snore.

What had he said?

Doughnut weaves lee?

Dunes need meat?

Once her mind solved the riddle, Paisley's eyelids jolted open. *Don't leave me…*

On the nightstand, her cell buzzed. Since the caller ID said it was her mother, Paisley ignored it.

PAISLEY WOKE TO a view that might have been on another world. Thick fog rose from the valley, yet the rising sun bathed emerald pastures and red rock spires in an ethereal glow. In the distance, Mount Rockwell's crown of snow glistened.

The baby kicked, and she smiled, covering the tender spot with her hand, then turning to Wayne, wanting to share the joyful moment and view. Only Wayne was no longer there.

It was no easy feat to roll over, but sure enough, by the time she accomplished the chore, she found the side of the bed he'd occupied vacant.

Don't leave me…

What had he meant?

For a sworn bachelor, his request made no sense. But for a man who was lonely and tired and appreciative of the companionship they'd slipped into and the comfort that brings? Yeah, she could see a sort of twisted logic to that.

But for how long?

And how did she guard herself against the same issues?

The more they were together, the more she found herself wanting *more*. Not acceptable, considering her son deserved the kind of man who wanted a lifelong commitment—not to indefinitely hang out as long as it was fun. Comfortable. What happened when it wasn't? When challenging times inevitably hit? Sleep deprivation and fevers and juggling a myriad of baby care activities with work?

Paisley forced a deep breath.

A knock sounded on her door. *Wayne?*

"Good morning—oh yay, you're up." Jules entered with a wooden tray. "The guys are already off for a trail ride, so I figured while it's still quiet around here we could fit in my world-famous homemade cinnamon rolls and girl talk."

"Mmm… Thank you." Paisley pushed herself higher

in the bed, smoothing her hair back into its ponytail holder. "I could have made it to the kitchen. You didn't have to go to this trouble."

Jules waved off Paisley's concerns. "It's my pleasure."

She set the tray on the bedside table. It not only held two saucers with forks and ooey, gooey rolls, but steaming floral cups filled with tea and a vase containing three sweet-smelling lilies.

"You're not allergic, are you? To the flowers?"

"Not at all. They're lovely. Thanks."

"The tea is caffeine-free. Peppermint." Jules distributed the food and drinks, then sat with a smiling sigh in the nearest of a pair of pastel armchairs in front of the window. "Wayne says you're due in two months?"

"I am."

"Nervous? Excited? Scared? All of the above?" Wayne's mom sipped her tea.

"For sure, the last option." She wished she could truly open up to the kindhearted woman about how terrified she was by the prospect of becoming a single mother. "All of my clients with kids say once they arrive, maternal instincts kick in, and I'll know what to do."

"Sort of?" Jules said with a pinched laugh. "I remember telling my mom and grandmother that Peter and I didn't need any help after leaving the hospital. I'd read stacks of parenting books and thought I knew it all. Well, we weren't in the apartment above the barn five minutes before Wayne started squalling. Peter and I took one look at each other, and I swear in unison we both blurted to call in the cavalry. My mom and grand-mother helped a lot during those first weeks. It was hard, but in the end, when you first hold your sweet baby in your arms... There's nothing in the world quite like it. Although, I suppose holding my first grandchild will come awfully close." Jule's wistful smile broke Paisley's heart. She didn't want to carry on this lie a moment longer, and fought a flash of resentment toward Wayne for ever having made her. But that wasn't fair. She'd volunteered for this mission and was honor bound to see it through.

"Not to change the subject," Paisley said after finishing her roll, "but is Peter feeling up to being on horseback?"

"Of course. Why wouldn't he be? And what's with all the questions about his health? He just had his yearly physical last month, and bragged about having better cholesterol and blood pressure marks than me—and I'm five years younger than him."

"Really?" Oh boy. Guilt consumed her for feeling bad over seriously great news.

Jules set her cup on the whitewashed table between the chairs. "I probably don't want to know the answer to this, but how about you do me a big favor and let me in on what's going on?"

"I, um..." Paisley held her teacup up to her mouth. "I'm not sure what you mean."

"Sure, you do. Why does my son keep treating his father with kid gloves? And why do you seem as tense as a cat stuck on a tin roof in a lightning storm?"

"That would be a bad spot..." Paisley found a faint

smile, before hugging her baby for much-needed strength.

"Paisley, *please*." Jules rose from her chair to perch on the edge of the bed, and placed her weathered hand over her own. The sensation was so warm, so unexpected and quintessentially mothering in the sort of way Paisley had never known that she fell a little further under the woman's spell. "Tell me if there's something going on between Peter and my son."

Paisley wanted to come clean, but because she'd promised Wayne that no matter what, she wouldn't reveal their scheme, Paisley wrapped Jules in a fierce hug, telling the woman the only truth she knew. "When it comes to Wayne and his dad, all I can tell you is that they share a very special bond."

One I pray lasts a whole lot longer...

Chapter Nine

"Have you ever seen a more gorgeous place?" Amid workers scurrying to set up tables and chairs, Monica tossed her white straw hat into the clear mountain air, spinning in slow motion with her long, dark hair streaming behind her as if she were in a shampoo commercial. If Paisley didn't love her so much, she'd have thrown up a little in her mouth.

"It's a spectacular setting for a wedding." Paisley gave her in-need-of-a-wash ponytail a self-conscious tug. Why hadn't she put on her new cowboy hat before leaving her room? At least her feet felt comfy in her boots. "Where's Logan?"

"Where do you think? He and Wayne took off on horses. I've never seen two grown men who are more inseparable." Hands on her hips, Monica shook her head. "There are SEALs flying in from all over the country. One thing's for sure, I should have the safest guests of any bride on the planet."

"True." It felt good to laugh, but in the back of her mind there was always the truth of why she was here. For Peter. The thought was as tragic as it was inconceivable. She honestly hoped he was faking. The fall-out from that would be far less tragic than him dying.

She swallowed the instant knot in her throat.

Standing between the century-old barn and the hacienda ranch house, Paisley could all too easily see herself and her baby boy living out their happily-ever-after on this magical place.

He'd get such a kick out of the horses and cattle and off-key rooster that hadn't quite gotten the memo that the sun had risen a few hours earlier. Was the bull snorting at every worker hustling past his wooden fence the famous Bruce?

The fact that her son would never see any of this made her even more sad.

"Aw, Paise…" Monica rushed toward her for a hug. "What's wrong? You can't be pouty when we're shopping for your dress. The guys should be back soon. Maybe we should see if Jules wants to tag along?"

"No! Sorry to snap, but the last thing I want is for poor Jules to be any more disappointed when she learns the truth. I'm stunned Peter hasn't told her he's sick."

"Not cool."

"I know, right? When I think about sweet Jules running this massive place all by herself…" Paisley shook her head, too overcome with pregnancy hormones to even try explaining how awful she'd felt earlier about essentially lying to Jules.

Monica led her to a wooden bench beneath a live oak. Even the tree was perfect. And the bench. "Jules & Peter" had been carved into the backrest's upper rung, along with the date of their wedding anniversary.

Paisley cried harder.

"You're freaking me out. Sit." Monica gave her a gentle nudge onto the seat. "Since I'm in all white, I'll stand. But quit blubbering and tell me what's wrong."

"You're a horrible friend. I'm not blubbering. A-and you try carrying Dr. Dirtbag's baby all by yourself—it's not a piece of cake." She stopped her rant long enough to blow her nose on the tissue Monica had found in her white Chanel purse. "I'm starving, though. And would love a piece of cake."

Monica laughed. "Honey, we'll get you a whole cake. Now, take some deep breaths, and then tell me what's wrong."

"F-for starters, Wayne and I kissed."

"Really? I need details…"

"I-it was wonderful. For me, at least. But I don't think he l-liked it. And now that I've seen how amazing this place is, I can't stop wondering what it might be like if Wayne wanted me for real. But that's just silly, since I'm not his type."

"Stop." Hands on her hips, Monica frowned. "That's crazy talk. You're pretty and smart and supersweet— any man would be lucky to have you."

"Y-you're just saying that to be nice."

"You know me better than that. I always tell the truth. You, my angel—" Monica kissed the top of her head "—are a saint. Wayne would be lucky to have you. And with all this kissing going on, who knows? Maybe you two will get married for real? Stranger things could happen."

Paisley snorted. "I have more faith in a pending alien

Dear Reader,

IT'S A FACT: if you answer 4 quick questions, we'll send you **4 FREE REWARDS!**

I'm not kidding you. As a leading publisher of women's fiction, we value your opinions… and your time. That's why we are prepared to **reward** you handsomely for completing our mini-survey. In fact, we have 4 Free Rewards for you, including 2 free books and 2 free gifts.

As you may have guessed, that's why our mini-survey is called **"4 for 4".** Answer 4 questions and get 4 Free Rewards. It's that simple!

Thank you for participating in our survey,

Pam Powers

To get your 4 FREE REWARDS:
Complete the survey below and return the insert today to receive 2 FREE BOOKS and 2 FREE GIFTS guaranteed!

"4 for 4" MINI-SURVEY

1 Is reading one of your favorite hobbies?
☐ YES ☐ NO

2 Do you prefer to read instead of watch TV?
☐ YES ☐ NO

3 Do you read newspapers and magazines?
☐ YES ☐ NO

4 Do you enjoy trying new book series with FREE BOOKS?
☐ YES ☐ NO

YES! I have completed the above Mini-Survey. Please send me my 4 FREE REWARDS (worth over $20 retail). I understand that I am under no obligation to buy anything, as explained on the back of this card.

235/335 HDL GMYE

FIRST NAME	LAST NAME

ADDRESS

APT.#	CITY

STATE/PROV.	ZIP/POSTAL CODE

over again, she pointed toward Monica's ridiculously flat tummy. "How far along are you?"

"Only a few weeks. You're the first one besides Logan I've told. But stop being a depressing pregnant lady, because with all the activities we have planned between now and tomorrow night, I can't be constantly redoing my makeup because of tears."

Laughing, crying, Paisley nodded.

How was it possible to be so happy for her dear friend, yet so sad and scared for herself? The worst part was, she didn't fully understand why. She'd been independent for a long time. Why was she flipping out now?

Probably in large part because ever since she and Wayne had launched their fake engagement, he'd been helpful and attentive and showered her with the sort of male perfection she'd only ever seen in magazine articles or her fertile imagination.

He was amazing. But he also wasn't really hers.

Her heart struggled to make the distinction.

WAYNE WANTED—NO, NEEDED—to talk to Paisley, but Monica and Logan's wedding mayhem was seriously screwing any chance of him getting alone time.

He and his father hadn't spoken since their time on the trail. Judging by the way he hunched in his saddle, something for sure wasn't right. Peter took tremendous pride in sitting tall on his horse. Since then, his dad had been slow moving with unsaddling the horses and getting them brushed and fed. But after a brief rest, he'd seemed in his element while showing off his prized ancient barn and award-winning cattle breeding operation to the men in Monica's family.

As soon as Logan arrived, Wayne had hit the trail again with a fresh mount.

Logan and his father, Keith—a retired fire chief from North Carolina—couldn't get enough majestic western scenery.

According to Logan, that afternoon he and Monica were supposed to take Paisley to get her wedding dress. After which, Monica had a full schedule for Paisley and all the other women in attendance—massages and manicures and pedicures. Anyway, he was glad Paisley was being pampered. She deserved it.

After his second ride of the day and caring for the horses, Wayne was wiped.

Too bad for him that Paisley and Monica waited just outside the barn for him and Logan, pouncing as soon as they exited.

"It's about time," Monica said. "Geez, Wayne, do you expect your bride to meet you at the altar in her pj's?"

"Lay off him," Logan said. "He's had a rough day."

"So have I. And think of poor Paise who's hours from her pretend wedding day and still has no dress."

"Sorry." Wayne draped his arms over Paisley's shoulders, drawing her close to kiss her cheek. "Let me grab my truck keys, then we'll go. I know the perfect place."

"No truck," Monica said. "I've got a limo standing by." She pointed toward the white stretch model that

Bruce the bull stared down as if it wasn't sure whether he wanted to attack it or make sweet bull love to it.

Wayne balked. "Do you have any idea how ridiculous we're going to look pulling up to the Pine Ridge Thrift Emporium in *that*?"

"Wait a second—you're buying Paisley her wedding gown at a thrift store? I thought you had something nicer in mind, or I would have taken her back in San Diego."

"Sorry. I had a lot on my mind. She'll find a great dress at the thrift store."

"Over my dead and bloated body."

"That could be arranged," Wayne mumbled under his breath.

"Watch it," Logan said with a growl. "Surely, there's a nice dress shop around?"

"Not unless you want to head to Phoenix?"

"How far is that?" Monica asked.

Wayne shrugged. "It's a good ways down the road. Like a few hours."

"Please, quit bickering," Paisley said. "A thrift store dress is fine. It's not like it's going to be a treasured keepsake."

"But it could be," Monica pointed out. "If a certain someone would take his head out his derriere long enough to—"

"That's enough out of both of you." Logan led his bride-to-be toward the waiting limo. "Paisley, I'm sorry your special dress shopping outing has turned into a pissing war between these two, but we'll make it better." He held open the limo's rear door for her.

Wayne brushed aside his supposed best friend. "I'll get her door. And for the record, this thrift shop is awesome. You'll love it."

The condemning stares of his fake fiancée, his supposed best friend and Monica left Wayne doubting his words...

WITH HELP FROM Wayne and Logan, Paisley managed to squeeze into the massive vehicle. The white leather seats formed a horseshoe with Monica and Logan seated nearest the driver, and Paisley and Wayne facing forward from the rear. The roof had been outfitted with tiny lights that twinkled to the beat of Monica's country love song playlist.

It was hard watching true love play out before her. Monica and Logan shared the sort of real commitment Paisley had always wanted. In no way did she begrudge them their happiness. She just felt a sad twinge for herself and her son for the fact that he would most likely grow up without a father.

When Monica and Logan embarked on a make-out session, Paisley forced herself to look away. Clearing her throat, she asked Wayne, "How was your ride with your dad?"

"Good. But bittersweet. I could tell he wasn't feeling his best. It made me feel better about our sham. Mom won't like it, but for Dad, we're giving him the ultimate gift. After our ride, I don't think he's faking." His voice shook as he said, "I'm not ready to lose him." He took her hand, smoothing his thumb over her palm, in the process flooding her with an achy warmth that had less to do with physical awareness, but the sort of soul-deep, lifelong connection she craved. "Thank you for being here for me. I don't deserve you."

"I—I'm glad to help."

"Being back on the land was a treat." Still holding her hand, he leaned his head back and sighed. "Big skies. Views for miles. I want to get you on a horse."

"You do know I can't ride?"

"Well, sure, maybe not now, but eventually."

"I don't mean to be cruel, but once your dad passes, I probably won't be back to your ranch."

A shadow passed over his handsome features. Was it possible the realization of their pending separation made him as sad as it did her?

For the remainder of the trip, while Logan and Monica smooched and whispered and giggled, Paisley pretended all was right in her world. She pretended Wayne's sudden brooding silence didn't bother her and that she'd always dreamed of finding her wedding gown in a thrift store. But, then, what did it matter? This was just a dress—nothing meant to last a lifetime. Just like her pretend relationship with the man still holding her hand.

"You okay?" she finally asked.

"Sure. Just tired." He glanced her way. When their gazes met, the collision of their connection was enough to force her to look away. How was it possible that for years they'd been friends, yet only now did she feel as if she was truly seeing him?

"I have a question."

"Shoot."

"If the ranch is your happy place, what in the world are you doing in San Diego?"

He released her hand.

"Never mind." The sudden stern set of Wayne's expression told Paisley her question struck a nerve. "It's none of my business."

"No. Considering we're supposed to be married, it's fair game." He rubbed his forehead. "The truth is that I didn't know what I had till it was gone. Don't get me wrong—I love being in the navy, but I'd be lying if I told you I don't miss my family and the feel of dirt beneath my boots."

"Why not retire? I'm sure after your dad passes, your mom could use your help."

Lips pressed in a grim line, he nodded.

"I'm sorry. I didn't mean to bring down the mood. Wedding dress shopping should be fun." Hoping to restore their usual lighthearted banter, she flashed a smile.

"It's cool."

That was the last cryptic thing he said for the thirty minutes it took to bump over the remainder of the ranch's dirt road.

On smooth blacktop, with Monica and Logan deep in their own cozy world, Paisley said, "If we're going to do this—make a convincing couple for your parents—I can't deal with you going silent. I understand what you're facing with your dad is beyond heavy, but I've got my own issues." Out of habit, she pressed her palms to her baby.

"Sorry. My head is exploding."

"Did you take something? I would usually have ibuprofen in my purse, but with the baby—"

"Thanks, but it's not the kind of pain a few pills can manage. I'm screwed up in here." He pressed his hand to his chest. "Part of me wants to ask my CO for emergency leave, but another part doesn't want to let down my team—which must sound ridiculous to an outsider, but my teammates are my brothers. I love them every bit as much as my family. I can't let them down."

"Don't you think they'd understand?"

He ran his fingers along a seam in the seat's upholstery. "I'm sure they would. It's just complicated."

"Tell me about it," she said with a half smile. "But maybe that's why fate brought us together? You help me with grocery runs and finding my shoes. I help you sort the complexities of being there for everyone you love."

"Paisley Carter…" He arched his head back and sighed, then fixed her with a magnetic stare she was incapable of escaping. He reached out to her, trailed his fingers over her jaw. His touch was innocent, yet erotic. Ordinary, yet inexplicably complex. "One day you are going to make some lucky SOB an amazing wife." He took her hand in his, bonding them, palm against palm. The simple gesture resulted in a tightening in Paisley's chest, as well as a swelling knot in her throat.

Paisley wasn't sure how to respond.

With Dr. Dirtbag, she'd had her life planned down to Saturday morning treks to the farmer's market and spending rainy Sundays in bed. His rejection made her feel no more valuable than roadside litter. The fact that Wayne temporarily found her of value upped her status from mere garbage to a recycled good, but she'd only be useful until his father's passing. Sure, she was doing Wayne a favor, but it was proving surprisingly tough on her self-esteem. She'd already been discarded by her parents; was she mentally tough enough to carry on the tradition by being tossed by a second man?

During the final ten minutes to Pine Ridge, she was the silent one.

The population sign boasted 853, but she was dubious as to where those citizens might be. The place was as empty as a ghost town. There was only one road, flanked on either side by an assortment of businesses, including competing beauty parlors, a drugstore, a diner and Realtor. The structures were a ragtag mix of adobe and faded wood. But flower boxes brimming with yellow blooms the gardener wannabe in her thought were called Blue Haze Spurge made for an overall cohesive and welcoming look. Weathered blond brick sidewalks looked as if they'd been there a hundred years, as did the black wrought iron gaslights.

After a brief pause at the lone stoplight, they were rolling again. A trio of little boys caught sight of the flashy car and tore off down the sidewalk, their frowning mother running after them.

Paisley hugged her baby bump, dreaming of the day her boy was big enough to run and play and picture himself riding in a fancy car.

The limo slowed before turning into the lot of a cement block behemoth of a store.

Monica gaped out her window. "No, no, no. Are you

seriously taking my best friend wedding dress shopping in a repurposed grocery store?"

"It's okay." Paisley swallowed the knot in her throat—not because she didn't enjoy a great thrift store find, but because she wished for more of an authentic wedding experience. A beautiful boutique like the one where Monica found her gown. A mother weeping with joy. Saleswomen pouring champagne and parading her in front of mirrors. Most of all, Paisley wanted the real man—the real love—all of that pomp implied. "This is for Peter. He'll never know where we found my dress. What matters is that our marriage brought him peace."

"You're a better person than me," Monica said.

"True," Wayne quipped.

"Watch it," Logan warned. "Kindly be respectful to my bride."

"You mean your pit bull?"

Logan laughed.

Monica smacked him.

"Sorry, babe." He thoroughly kissed her. "You can be fierce."

After another glare at Wayne, she said to Logan, "I'll take that as a compliment." To Paisley she asked, "Sweetie, are you sure this is what you want?"

Of course not!

But she'd promised Wayne, so Paisley nodded.

Once the limo driver turned off the engine, then rounded the vehicle to open the rear door, they all piled out to stand on a cracked and stained concrete lot. The day was sunny with an annoying wind. Wayne's family ranch was nestled into the mountains, but the town was located on a lonely stretch of desert land that had more rusty-red sand than green anything.

Wayne asked, "Ready to find you the perfect dress?"

She winced. "I suppose."

He squeezed her hand, infusing her with a restless, achy yearning to one day be a real bride who wasn't just needed, but thoroughly loved and cherished.

For now, she'd have to settle for being a real friend.

Presumably to keep her from tripping on the uneven pavement, Wayne slipped his arm around her waist. To onlookers, she supposed they appeared like a happy couple. In her heart, she felt like an imposter. Never had she been more keenly aware of how deeply she longed for a true companion for herself and father for her baby.

Chapter Ten

For the moment in time when Wayne left her to open
the door of the converted former grocery store, Paisley
felt ridiculously bereft without him.

What was she doing here?

How had her life gotten so out of control?

The enormous space featured row upon row of
clothes, books, household goods and furniture. Reg-
gae played over the intercom and hand-drawn signs
hung from the ceiling, declaring this week's special—
in celebration of Beach Week, all items with green and
blue tags were 50 percent off.

She'd be hard-pressed to imagine a place more removed from the shore.

"Maybe we'll get lucky and find you a bargain
gown," Wayne said.

"Great." She blew him an acid kiss. "Not only do I
have a fake fiancé, but he's cheap."

"I'm saving up for our imaginary honeymoon."

"Uh-huh…" While Monica and Logan veered toward a vintage jewelry display, Paisley waddled to the
women's clothing section where she found a surpris-

ingly great selection of gowns. From simple to elaborate, beaded or lacy or both, surely, she'd find something that worked.

"What kind of style were you thinking?" Wayne asked. He pulled a white sequined number with peekaboo cutouts at the belly and lower back. "How about this? Your baby bump could stick out the hole."

She hoped her slit-eyed glare conveyed the full depth of her distaste for his ridiculous suggestion.

"It could be the perfect solution," he persisted.

"Keep it up. You'll be needing a good divorce attorney."

"Ouch." He clutched his chest, but returned the offensive garment to the rack from whence it came.

She swiped through dozens of gowns—white and ivory, satin and velvet and a shockingly ugly tan corduroy number that was so tacky it would have made for an awesome Halloween- or '60s-themed party costume. Gown after gown just didn't seem right. Too long or too short sleeves. Too many beads or not enough. Was she being too choosy for a dress that would only be worn to a pretend ceremony?

"Got it," Wayne announced from behind her. His radiant heat did little to soothe her already frayed nerves. "Close your eyes."

"Really?" She didn't even want to imagine the horror of what he was no doubt on the verge of showing her.

"Yes. Do it."

More because she knew he'd never shut up if she didn't, Paisley squeezed her eyes shut. Cutting off her vision heightened her other senses. When he stepped around her, a whisper of warm air caressed her forearms and heated cheeks. She smelled his faint citrus aftershave. From somewhere nearby a little girl giggled and for a crazy instant, she wondered if the noise had come from the childlike hope in her heart for this to one day be real. Shopping for the perfect wedding dress with her perfect fiancé.

"Open them."

She did. And then opened her mouth, only to quickly close it, swallowing the knot lurking at the back of her throat. He'd done it—found her the perfect gown. The gown she might have chosen even if she weren't as big as a house or shopping in a thrift store.

"Well?" He wagged the garment on its hanger. "What do you think?" The empire waist vision featured a boat neck with three-quarter sleeves. Thick brushed satin fabric made it feel rich. The vintage lace and crystal belt that would ride above her baby bump made it appear custom-made for her very pregnant body. "I like how it's elegant and not over-the-top. It suits you. It's simple, yet refined."

"Oh, really?"

He busted out laughing. "Sorry. I'm pretty sure I heard that line on a luxury car commercial, but it also seems fitting for this occasion. Try it on."

She snatched it from him, walking in her awkward gait toward a bank of dressing cubicles.

"Need help?" he asked, hot on her trail.

"I don't think so. But you'll be first on my list if I do."

"Cool." He sat on a blue plaid recliner that was

marked $39.99. "This is a pretty good deal. Think I should grab it for my apartment?"

"Absolutely. Especially since I won't be living there." She ducked into the dressing room without catching his reaction.

Even with the door closed behind her, the opening at the bottom left her feeling exposed. She'd worn her stupid hot pink capris again—mostly because anything else that fit was dirty. Monica's extreme dislike for them made Paisley wonder what Wayne thought. Was he out there now, judging the size of her *cankles* from his new recliner?

She managed to get undressed on her own, placing her voluminous pale pink maternity top on a bench beside the offensive capris.

With the wedding gown off the hanger, she was pleased to find the zipper opened low enough for her to step into the garment. She pulled it up and was more than a little thrilled to find the romantic rhinestone belt riding perfectly atop her bump. The bodice hugged her breasts in the right places and the long sleeves hid the jiggly parts of her upper arms. She managed to get the zipper almost up, but then couldn't reach the rest of the way around.

"How's it going?" Wayne asked. His voice sounded muffled through the door.

She cracked it open. "Could you please finish zipping me?"

"Absolutely." He was up in a flash.

She turned her back to him. Some silly part of her didn't want him seeing her until the gown was fully in place. It wasn't a matter of him seeing skin, but vanity. She wanted him to catch the full effect of the heartbreakingly pretty gown. She wanted to see if he'd notice her as a woman? Or merely his giant pregnant neighbor who was doing him a solid?

When he trailed the backs of his fingers along her spine, she shivered.

"Cold?"

Too hot. They'd been friends for years. Why now all of the sudden was his every touch launching fireflies in her tummy? It was downright embarrassing.

"All set. Turn around so I get the full vision."

"I will, but just a minute." She pushed him back just far enough to shut the door in his face, then took a moment to fuss with her hair. She fumbled through her purse to add lipstick and fresh powder. When she next looked at herself, for once in a very long while, she liked the woman staring back. Maybe it was the heightened color her awareness for Wayne had raised in her cheeks, but she really did look like a blushing bride.

Even by Monica's demanding standards, this dress was Instagram worthy.

Wayne pounded on the door. "I wanna see."

She forced a smile, then faced him, holding her breath, wanting, wishing, *aching* for his reaction to be anything other than—

"Cool. It fits. Now we need to find you one of those veil things and a bouquet. Want real flowers or will this do?" He reached behind him to the table next to his recliner, then handed her a ghastly silk floral bouquet that looked as if it had been made to match that corduroy dress.

"My florist already made her a legit one." Hands on her hips, Monica cast Wayne her trademark glare. "Sweetie, I can't believe I'm saying this about a thrift store wedding dress, but you look stunning. Just—wow."

"Thank you." Paisley hugged her friend, grateful for the second positive opinion, but it wasn't enough. Ridiculously, it was Wayne's approval she sought.

"Monica, have your people send me the bill." He made a spinning motion to Paisley. "Let me get the zipper for you. Then, while you're dressing, I'll find someone to ask if they can hold the recliner till I can get back with my truck."

"You're actually buying it?"

"You think I shouldn't? It's a steal." He'd already turned his back on her.

"Wayne…" She held her breath. *Say something! Anything! About me—not your stupid recliner.*

"Yeah?"

"Nothing." Why did her throat ache from the effort of holding back tears? He wasn't worth them.

"You sure? You look flushed."

"I'm good."

"Cool. Logan and I will meet you two at the check-out."

Once again ensconced in the dressing room, Paisley forced herself and her stupid hormones not to cry. *Cool?* The only word he could think of to sum up her beautiful gown and their swiftly approaching nuptials was *cool*?

Her stupid cell rang. Why wouldn't her mom stop? Lord knew, Paisley had enough on her plate in dealing with her uncertain future. No way was she emotionally equipped to tackle her rocky past.

She stepped out of the garment and hastily redressed in her work clothes.

"Need help?" Monica asked from outside the cramped space.

"No, thank you."

"If you do need me, I'll be in kitchenware. Don't tell Wayne I said this, but they have some incredible deals on vintage silver serving platters and candleholders. I want to grab polish and do before and after shots for an Instagram story."

"Perfect. I'll meet you over there."

Could this afternoon get any worse?

Honestly, what had she expected? For Wayne to catch one look at her in the surprisingly dreamy dress and declare his eternal love? She of all people ought to know relationships didn't work that way.

In fact, for her? They *never* worked that way.

She had to face it, no matter how badly she wanted to marry and settle down, the only guy in her future would be her son.

DAMN.

If someone had told Wayne he would be turned on by a pregnant lady in a wedding dress, he'd have told them they were three grenades shy of a full crate. Then he'd caught his first sight of Paisley in a wedding dress—his pick, no less—and all bets were off. He'd always thought she was pretty, but in that fancy number, she'd sported an ethereal glow.

She was an angel—*his* angel.

By the time he'd found a clerk to call for backup on his recliner, Wayne had discreetly adjusted his fly and reprimanded himself for wondering about pretend honeymoon logistics. Just in case, maybe he needed to Google pregnant lady sex positions?

Get your head out of the gutter!

His conscience snapped him back to reality.

This was Paisley he was talking about. And he was done thinking of her in any way other than strictly platonic. She and her baby deserved a real husband, and that was something he'd never again be.

He caught sight of her zigzagging around the obstacle course of other shoppers while trying to keep her dress's hem from touching the ground. A protective streak propelled him into action.

"Let me get that." He took the garment from her.

"Whew. Thanks. Who would have guessed a few yards of fabric and sparkle weigh a ton?"

"No kidding, right?" The gown might as well have been made of tissue. He settled it in the crook of his right arm. His left arm he eased around her shoulders, steering her toward the checkout line, telling himself it was common courtesy bringing out the gentleman in him as opposed to the proprietary notion that if they'd met in another time or place, she might be carrying his baby. The thought was at first exhilarating, then terrifying. How much worse could the mess with Chelsea have been if they'd had a child?

Wayne paid for the dress, decided now probably wasn't the best time to buy a recliner, then pitched in to help Logan haul all of Monica's finds to the limo.

"Have something to say to me?" he asked her once the trunk was closed.

"Nope." She ducked into the vehicle's open rear door.

"Monica, come on," Logan defended his friend. "Wayne did pull through with this place."

"True. Wish it was back in San Diego. Some of that silver was pretty enough I felt guilty for paying so little—especially, when this is a nonprofit charity to support kids."

"So what was it want to say to me?" Wayne badgered.

"Sorry," Monica said to Wayne with a begrudging tone. "You were right. But for the record, you got lucky on the dress."

"See?" Logan kissed his bride. "This is great. My two best friends on the planet finally getting along. It's the wedding gift I've always wanted."

When Wayne and Monica both growled, Paisley laughed. It kinda pissed him off that she wasn't on his side.

But then she fell asleep on the ride home, resting her head on his shoulder, sweetly snoring and smelling of lilacs. How could he stay mad when all he wanted to do was protect her and keep her comfortable and happy—all highly conflicting emotions for a guy embarking on a fake marriage.

By the time they reached the ranch, Monica swept Paisley off to prepare for the wedding rehearsal.

While grabbing a quick shower, prepping himself for a night of more pretending and lies, Wayne found himself dreading everything to come aside from being with Paisley. The more he thought about it, the more he realized what an incredibly special woman she was to have gone along with this charade.

Heading over to the barn, he waited to walk with his dad. His mom had gone early to get all dolled up with the other women.

"How are you feeling?" Wayne asked.

"Good, good." His dad patted Wayne's back. "I am sore from horse ride, but thinking about wedding and baby make me strong. For them—for you and your momma, I want live forever." Tears shone in his eyes.

Wayne's heart squeezed like a fist.

"What does your doctor say?"

Peter waved off the question. "He know nothing. He say I have cancer and that all I hear. It bad. Very bad."

"But, Dad, aren't you getting treatment? Cancer isn't always the death sentence it used to be. Thousands are cured every day."

"I no cure. Don't tell your momma. It break her heart."

That explained a lot. Another suspicion confirmed. His dad really hadn't told his mom. No wonder she'd acted so normal. She had no idea of the magnitude of the secret her husband was keeping.

"Dad…" Wayne stopped him before they'd reached the massive Pinyon pine and iron front door. "You can't keep this from her. It's wrong. Cruel. She deserves to know."

"How do I tell woman I love goodbye?" Wayne's dad showed his age and poor health by all but collapsing onto the entry hall bench. "The pain of that kill me before cancer."

Fighting to keep it together, Wayne asked, "Would you at least let me talk to your doctor? Maybe something's getting lost in translation?"

Peter shrugged. "If you must. But it make no difference."

"It might. After the wedding, we'll go—together. It's about time you let me shoulder some of this burden."

His dad's head was bowed, but he nodded. "Yes. I suppose that is good."

Together, they took their time walking to the barn.

It was inconceivable to Wayne that his once strapping father was now a shell of his former self. On the surface, he seemed healthy enough, but the more little things he noticed, the more his diagnosis added up. His difficulty that morning in his saddle. His sagging shoulders and defeated attitude. At least he'd agreed to finally allow Wayne to be involved in his recovery.

It might not buy more time, but maybe it would?

In which case, that opened a whole new can of proverbial worms with Paisley. But would staying pretend married to her be all bad?

IF ANY WOMAN was more of a ballbuster than Monica, it was her wedding planner. Over and over they rehearsed their placement at the altar and the women took turns walking down the aisle. He didn't like the stern set of Paisley's normally upbeat expression.

He supposed it was selfish of him to expect her to put on even more of a show for his folks than she already was, but it would have been nice to at least once see her smile.

Finally, with the practice vows behind them, and a long night of dinner and toasts ahead, he got a second alone with his pretend bride.

"How are you holding up?" he asked while waiting their turn to climb into one of the three horse-drawn wagons transporting guests and family. On the itinerary Monica distributed, this was supposed to have been an old-fashioned hayride, but the seats lining the white wagons were upholstered in white and the wheels festooned with vines and flowers. Even the white horses' manes had been braided with flowers. "This is turning out to be an even bigger spectacle than I'd imagined."

"No kidding, right?" She hid a yawn behind her hand. "I'd love a nap, but the show must go on."

He leaned close, whispering into her ear, "Speaking of shows, I just want to thank you again. I had a talk with my dad, and the two of us—the baby—are making him happy. He even said he'd allow me to join him on his next doctor visit."

"Thank goodness." Her sigh sounded as if she'd carried the weight of nearby Monument Valley between her shoulders. "Your mom brought me breakfast in bed, then drilled me about why we both seemed concerned with Peter's health. I didn't let anything slip, but I'm guessing if he's as sick as he claims, he won't be able to hide it much longer. I didn't have the heart to pile it on by admitting her new daughter-in-law is also a big, fat liar."

Wayne shoved his hands in his jeans pockets. "Yeah, well, her son is, too. Which is why I have to ask—are you sure about this? You've heard his crap English. If I go to his next appointment and learn there are viable treatment options he's ignored, that might mean he makes a full recovery. You didn't sign on for that. If you want to back out, I understand." He took her hand and stroked her palm with his thumb, praying, hoping, holding his breath for her response.

Paisley groaned. "Wayne, keeping this lie is hard. Of course, I want to help your dad in any way I can, but—"

"There you two are!" Monica had a glowering Jules and Peter in tow, along with a woman Paisley assumed was the official event photographer, judging by the three cameras strapped around her neck and four terrified-looking assistants. "I want to get a family photo before the sun sets."

"I no like picture," Peter said.

Jules said, "I prefer to have my portrait taken with just my son and daughter-in-law."

"What's going on?" Wayne asked low enough for only his parents to hear.

His mother wiped tears. "Imagine my surprise when I dashed back to the house for my lipstick and heard you two talking in the entry hall. How could you—both of you—keep this from me? Peter? You have cancer?"

Wayne's heart stopped.

Chapter Eleven

"No," his father said. "Horse have it. Not me. You mis-heard."

"I'm pretty sure I didn't. If something's seriously wrong with you, Peter, I have a right to know."

His dad cast Wayne a beseeching look. One that begged him to hold tight to his dignity at least a short while longer.

"Honest, Mom, Dad's fine. He was telling me how the vet thought Buttercup may be sick, but turns out she's healthy as a horse." *Cue forced chuckle.* "See? We're all good."

"But, Wayne," Paisley interjected. "Don't you think—"

Framing her lovely face with his hands, he kissed her quiet. "Let's go take a nice picture, then stuff our pieholes with beans and ribs and corn bread."

Looking wide-eyed and dazed—hopefully, from his kiss—Paisley asked, "How do you know that's what we're having?"

"Duh," Monica said, exchanging a look with Wayne.

She knew the score, and for supporting him, he'd cut her some slack. "It's on the itinerary. Are we good?"

"Perfect," Wayne said. "We'll catch up as soon as the photo's done."

Wayne held Paisley's arm as they trudged behind his parents to the lawn's farthest edge.

Bruce the bull gave them a snort on their way by.

Peter paused to rub the massive creature's snout.

Under his breath, Wayne said, "Mom's right. Dad does love that bull more than the rest of us combined."

"He does not. He's probably feeling like up until tonight, Bruce was his only confidant. But why didn't you use your mom overhearing your conversation to your advantage? You and your dad could have come clean about everything—even us. And what was that kiss?" Paisley demanded. "You're supposed to be stopping this madness. Not perpetuating it with more fake romance and lust and…and…starry dew dust."

"What exactly is 'starry dew dust'? I'm not familiar with that substance."

"Hush. You know exactly what I mean."

"I can guess. But are you trying to tell me you want out of our arrangement?" Waiting for her answer made his heart pound to an alarming degree.

"Honestly? I'm not sure what I want. But then I remembered the way your dad's gaze brightened when he felt the baby kick and when he sees the two of us together, and I can't bear to be the one who breaks his heart."

"So we're still good?"

She nodded. "But we shouldn't be. Someone's going

to get hurt. Me. You. Your mom and dad. We're playing a dicey game, Wayne. It's only a matter of time before we get caught."

"Unless we don't."

"What does that even mean?"

He wasn't sure. Maybe that he'd already known her for so long, and that he enjoyed being with her so much, kissing her so much, that despite his utter lack of faith in the whole concept of love, he felt something true and deep and frighteningly real for this friend who had somehow become more.

The photographer waved them over. "I'm going to need all four of you against the hedge. Mom, Dad, how about you frame the bride and groom. Then we'll get individual shots and mix and match pairings. Sound like a plan? Great! Let's do this!"

Assistants leaped to their marks.

Wayne was thrilled for the distraction. He and Paisley's talk had gotten way too heavy for his liking. It was in his best interest to keep all of this casual—at least as much as possible when faced with the undeniable fact that his father was dying.

Posed against Mount Rockwell and the valley and the sky in its orange, violet and blue splendor, Wayne somehow managed to smile through shot after shot. He'd made a solemn personal vow to never again marry, yet he found himself in the unfamiliar territory of wanting to always be with her. And her baby boy. Making him not only a husband, but instant dad.

Sweat popped out on his forehead.

His stomach turned queasy.

"Blotting! Groom needs blotting!" The photographer waved to a minion who burst into action by pressing a dry cloth to Wayne's face.

Wayne brushed the twentysomething kid aside. "I'm done."

"We still have a few more shots," the photographer said.

"Wayne, honey?" His mother chased after him. "Are you okay?"

"Leave boy alone!" Peter said. "He must learn be tough like man!"

"Hush! The last thing Paisley needs is stress."

"Let's call it a wrap." The photographer gestured for her crew to hurry.

Jules poked her finger at her husband's chest. "I'm still not sure I believe you and Wayne that you were talking about a horse. And now that I think about it, you haven't been yourself. I swear to God, if you truly are sick and haven't told me, I'll make you that much sicker myself. Over the course of our marriage, you've pulled some harebrained stunts, but if you have cancer and aren't telling me…" Her rage dissolved into sobs.

Peter pulled her into his arms. "I so sorry to worry you. I promise, I am very fine."

"Guys," Wayne said, "please, stop fighting. For Monica and Logan, for Paisley and myself, could you please put on happy faces and at least pretend you're having a wonderful time?"

"I try," Peter said. "But your momma… She test my patience."

"Me? Oh—that's rich." Jules swiped tears from her cheeks.

"Okay, great. So you're both working on family unity. I appreciate the effort. Paise? You and our giant baby ready to eat some ribs?" Wayne turned a one-eighty, but she was nowhere to be seen. "Paise?"

He angled the rest of the way only to find her gone.

"Where do you think she went?" his mother asked, voice laced with concern.

"No clue, but she can't have gone far. You two entertain our guests. I'll find her."

"Paise?"

"Go away!" Having run from the shame and embarrassment of the scene unfolding with Wayne's parents, Paisley had escaped to her room where she'd collapsed onto the bed. And now put a pillow over her head.

Maybe if Wayne couldn't see her, he'd go away?

"There you are."

No such luck.

"What's wrong? You're missing the barbecue." He removed the pillow, so she closed her eyes. "I know you're not sleeping."

"Am, too."

"I also know ribs happen to be one of your favorite foods."

"No. I'm allergic."

"You weren't that time a few years back when Logan had them catered poolside for our buddy Gideon's going away party." He smoothed his fingertips maddeningly up and down her bare upper arm. "If my memory serves me correctly, you ate at least three racks all by your lonesome. All my SEAL friends were in awe. They kept asking, 'Where did you find that human rib vacuum and where do I get one of my own?'"

"Stop it. I hate you." She summoned the energy to grab another pillow to put over her head.

"No, you don't." He joined her on the bed, big spoon to her little. "Come eat ribs with me. I'm sure Monica misses you."

"She probably doesn't even notice I'm gone. And, anyway, I can't keep watching you lie to your poor mom. She deserves better." Wriggling free of him, fighting to regain some small semblance of logic she couldn't seem to find whenever he held her in his arms, Paisley scooted up in the bed and rested her back against the pile of pillows. "Because I do have affection for you as a friend, I'm going to pretend not to have noticed your suddenly panicked expression. You were actually sweating with terror. Let me guess—you realized the lunacy of a fake marriage that lasts a few years rather than months."

"Maybe. Hell, I don't know." Whereas she'd moved up in the bed, he moved down, resting his head on the baby. "Think he hears me?"

"I think so. I read an article that said it's been proven babies are born recognizing their parents' voices."

"It could work, you know."

"What?"

"Us getting married. We'd at least know what we're getting into. Having both been burned at love, neither of us is in the market for another romance. But your little guy will need a dad and you could use the help. My parents stay happy—at least about us and the baby. No one's ever the wiser. I don't have to look for a new roommate when Logan leaves our place for Monica's. It's a win-win for all involved."

Paisley closed her eyes and groaned.

"What's wrong?"

What's wrong? she wanted to screech. Forcing a deep breath, she tried maintaining a civilized tone. "Here's the thing… What if I do want romance? What if I want passion and flowers and dancing and laughing and great sex and eating ice cream together with only one spoon?"

Silence.

"Exactly. That's why it's probably best if we come clean with your parents tonight. We'll go ahead and stand up for Monica and Logan at their wedding as planned, but after that, I'd like to head back to San Diego."

"Paise…" He rubbed her belly. She could have grounded her little guy for kicking. "Did you feel that? Even John Wayne Jr. knows we should make this engagement official. Let's get married for real."

"Did you lose your hearing on your last mission? What didn't you understand about all I just said? The thought of being trapped for the next fifty years in a platonic friendship is untenable. I don't want to marry a friend—well, I do, but you know what I mean. I want the total package. A friend and a lover."

"Those kisses were hot as hell. I never said anything about us being platonic." He kissed a trail up her neck while easing his hand beneath her blouse. She should have pushed him away, but didn't. Damn her body for its instant arousal. Nipples standing at attention, practically begging for his tongue. The V between her legs throbbing with moist heat. Her need for him was downright embarrassing. "Hell, yes, to sex."

"You're an idiot." She brushed him away and rolled off the bed, struggling to her feet. Standing before the window, she stared out at the lavender-and-plum sky. "This isn't about bedroom bingo, but the kind of deeper feelings that sustain a couple through stuff like your parents are currently going through. I guarantee that if we were to join them at the barbecue, they've already kissed and made up."

"You think?" He left the bed to sit in one of the chairs beside the window, hugging her waist, resting his stupid-handsome face on the baby. Wayne's proximity set off dozens of tingly proximity alarms. How could she physically and emotionally distance herself from him, when she craved getting closer?

Clearing her throat, Paisley said, "Your mother adores your dad. From all I've seen, he feels the same for her. That's the kind of marriage I want, Wayne. Thank you for your offer. I really do appreciate it. But we've been over this before. When—*if*—I do decide to marry, my son and I deserve a man like your father who's all-in. Yes, his keeping his cancer from your mom is horrible, but he's doing it out of love. Just like we pretended to be engaged with good intentions. But if there's anything we can learn from this, it's that two wrongs don't make a right."

She bowed her head, combing her fingers over Wayne's soft buzz cut. The knot in her throat had grown to the size of a baseball.

How easy it would be to agree to be his wife for as long as he'd have her. Her fears about being a single mom would be instantly appeased. But what happened when weeks turned into months of sharing a bed with him and breakfasts and play-fighting over the remote? They'd raise her baby together, and her son would grow up believing Wayne was his father, and every time she saw Wayne bathe him or blow raspberries on his tummy or wipe drool from his chin, she'd grow a little closer to falling for him—assuming she hadn't already. When he failed to ever return her affections, she would be in no way prepared to face unrequited love for the next fifty or sixty years. Even worse—only a few years until someone hotter or more fun came along.

"Wish you'd reconsider," Wayne said, kissing her baby bump. Weakening her carefully thought out resolve. "If we don't marry, think of how disappointing that would be to my folks."

"I'm sorry," Paisley somehow managed, removing her ring, reaching for his hand to place it on his palm. "But as much as I love Jules and Peter, marrying you strictly to please them is wrong. This deception is killing me, and keeping your dad's cancer from your mom is cruel. She deserves to know the whole truth."

"It's about time you got here, buddy." Logan patted the empty seat on the picnic table bench alongside him.

The table was filled with strangers who chattered up a storm. "Did you get that happygram text from the CO?"

"Yeah. How'd Monica take the news that we're shipping out next week?"

"I'm too scared to tell her. Figure I'll wait until after we get back to San Diego. No sense in ruining her big day."

"Wise man. I'll follow your lead—not that it matters." Wayne set his loaded plate and a beer on the red-and-white-gingham-covered table.

"What's that supposed to mean? And where've you been? You and Paisley sneak off for—"

"Knock it off. I'm not in the mood."

"Damn, boy. What forked-tongued scorpion bit your ass?"

"Point of fact—scorpions have stingers." He tipped his hat in the direction of Paisley who seemed to be having fun at her table with Monica and a bunch of her family, and even his parents who had, sure enough, made up and now fed each other bites of baked beans. "But when it comes to Paisley, hell, maybe she's got both."

"Whatever happened, she'll get over it."

"Not happening. The wedding's off. She even gave back her ring."

"Wait—she's so pissed at you that she broke off your *pretend* engagement?" Logan laughed so hard, he swallowed a bite of potato salad the wrong way and had to down his entire beer to quit coughing.

"Yuk it up, pal. Yuk it up." Wayne shoved his food away in favor of beer and glowering.

Everyone aside from him seemed to be having the greatest time.

Monica had thought of everything. A country band played on a makeshift stage. Couples danced and laughed beneath tiny white lights strung through aspens and cottonwoods. A chuckwagon provided plenty of food and a bar served probably too much liquor.

"In all seriousness," Logan said, leaning in so the guy next to him wouldn't hear, "what happened? Monica said Paisley denies it, but she's pretty sure she has a thing for you."

"I thought so, too. But about an hour ago, I asked her to marry me for real and she turned me down cold, then starts spewing all this crap about feelings and sharing ice cream with one spoon. I get that she's looking for the kind of solid commitment you and Monica share, but I can't offer that. I could be a great friend to her, though. And a dad to her baby." He chugged a good bit more of his beer. "I'm a good catch. I know we went into this because of my dad, but she'd be getting a pretty sweet deal."

"You didn't tell her that, did you?"

"No. Should I?" He pushed himself up. "Hell, I'll go tell her right now."

"Bad idea." Logan shoved him back down. "This situation calls for finesse. Way more than I have. Mind bringing Monica in on the situation?"

"Of course, I'd mind. This is my own personal business. You know what happened the last time I got hitched. My marriage to Chelsea was the equivalent of filling my heart with gunpowder, then lighting the fuse. The woman destroyed me. No way I'm letting it happen again."

"What if you already did?"

"Huh?" Wayne wrinkled his nose.

"Hear me out. What if you already fell for Paisley, but it happened so slow—like over a period of all the time we've lived next door—that you never even saw it coming? But now that you've had a taste of what it would be like to be a couple, you find yourself liking it. You might already be in love with her. But you're too scared to admit it."

Wayne finished his beer. "I'm not scared of shit." But maybe he was?

"Here's what I think," Logan said.

"I don't care what you think."

"Tough. Next time there's a slow song—because I've seen you dance to fast stuff, and that sight shouldn't ever be repeated—ask for her hand, then lead her around the dance floor nice and slow. Woo her a little."

Wayne rolled his eyes. "I'm a freakin' soldier. I don't know the first thing about wooing."

Logan clamped his hand over Wayne's shoulder. "Then you'd best start Googling. Otherwise, it's gonna be a long, lonely life."

Chapter Twelve

"Stop being stubborn," Monica scolded while Paisley ate her weight in ribs.

Paisley hated that Wayne had been right about her loving ribs. Even worse, she hated herself for fearing she just might have already fallen for him. If she had, how was she ever supposed to recover? Being neighbors, she saw him all the time. Plus, there would be dinners shared with Logan and Monica. Holiday parties shared with her baby boy and mutual friends.

"You know what this is, don't you?" Monica asked.

"No, but I'm sure you're going to tell me."

"This is the car birthday gift refusal all over again."

Paisley rolled her eyes. "Don't start."

"Oh—trust me, I'm started, and I intend to keep going. Deny it all you want, but you've been crazy for Wayne since we first laid eyes on his pecs and abs at your apartment complex's pool. Now the guy genuinely wants to marry you and you're turning him down? Nope. Not happening. I say you're defaulting back to your comfy old relationship fail-safe of claiming you don't want to use anyone or you'll be like your mom.

News flash—you couldn't be more unlike your mother if you tried."

Tears stung Paisley's eyes. "But what if I am like her? Make no mistake, I wanted to take Wayne up on his offer. It would be a dream come true to raise my baby with him. To have Wayne with me through every milestone. But if he's only there out of a sense of obligation, or to up the stakes in this lying game we started, then he has no business getting married. I'd be using him just as surely as if he were one of my mother's meal tickets."

"How are you using him if you love him?"

"I don't."

Monica sighed. "For the sake of conversation, let's say you do. How would you be using a man if you love him heart and soul? And did you ever stop to consider he might feel the same about you, but he's still gun-shy from his divorce? What if after the baby is born and you two live together for a few months, you settle into a blissful routine that results in a lifetime of shared happiness and devotion and—"

"I adore you, but please stop. Just because you and Logan are living out your fairy tale, doesn't mean the rest of us will ever get a turn."

Monica's voice softened. "When's the last time you saw her?"

"Mom?" Paisley's gaze widened. Why was her friend pouring more salt in an already gaping wound? "Last year? I don't remember. The airfare to Miami is expensive, and then we were so busy at the shop. I got pregnant. Now I'm too far along to fly."

"Do you think it might help to talk to her?"

"No. I don't even want to be in the same room with her. I'm mortified by what she's done. Why can't she be normal? Why couldn't she work hard like everyone else instead of being a user? If I did see her, what would I say?"

"What's in your heart? Might be cathartic."

"I don't know."

Logan and Wayne sauntered up. Both held beers.

"Dance with me, woman." Logan held out his hand to Monica.

"Do I look like a cave girl to you?" She smoothed her already perfect hair. "Ask again—this time, in a manner befitting a princess who by this time tomorrow will be your queen."

Paisley didn't try hiding her smile. She did hide her deep longing to share the same silly banter with Wayne.

Logan tossed back his beer, then showed his shrieking and laughing bride-to-be the true meaning of caveman by hefting her over his shoulder and onto the dirt-turned-dance floor.

"They seem happy," Wayne said, setting his longneck bottle on the table.

"They sure do." Paisley had been so deep into her conversation with her friend that she hadn't noticed the thinning crowd. At least a third of the older set must have already left for the nearby dude ranch where they were staying.

"Look, Paise…" Wayne bowed his head, kicking at a grass clump with the toe of his cowboy boot. "I'm sorry if I came across as a hard-ass, trying to steer you to my way of thinking."

"No apology necessary. We both went into this for the express intention of helping your father. Mission accomplished, right?"

"Not if you bail."

"Wayne…" She bowed her head. "Your mom already suspects what's going on. It's only a matter of time before she learns the whole truth. I'm sorry, but I'm having serious doubts as to whether this was ever a sane idea. The two of us—we…" *We couldn't be more different in terms of what we want for our futures. I want love and commitment. I don't have a clue what you want, and I suspect you don't, either.*

"Logan says I should level with you." He removed his hat. Fanned himself. Clamped his hat back on top of his head. Was he nervous?

"Okay?"

"What if I like you?"

"As a friend? Or *more*?" *Really? Are we back in fourth grade?*

He cleared his throat. "I think maybe more. I don't know. But you deserve to know. So that's why I don't know what to do. I want to take you out on that dance floor and hold you and kiss you. I can't wait to hold your hand through labor and the thought of you not inviting me to share in that special moment eats me alive. But in the same respect, what if you and I connect on that deeper level you get all fired up about, and then we fall apart? We both would have invested a lot of time and emotional energy into something that might not pan out. Not because either of us haven't tried, but—"

"I'd planned to confess to your parents tonight, but since they seem so happy, how about you and I mend fences with a dance. If the dance works out, we might share another. After that, I wouldn't mind falling asleep the same way we did last night. Does any of that sound good to you?"

He sharply exhaled. "All of the above. And the wedding? You're going to marry me?"

"No. Not until you can stand before me, hat in hand, admitting that you don't just like me, but *love* me."

"Fair enough." He nodded, scratching the stubble already shadowing his jaws. "I'm going to take that to mean you already do—love me?"

She shrugged. "Cowboy, you sure do talk a lot when all I asked you to do was dance."

WAYNE HELD PAISLEY as if there were no tomorrow, because he might not have the pleasure of them sharing another day.

That text from his CO had caught him off his game. Ordinarily, he was psyched by new deployments, but this time around, there was a hesitancy holding him back. He'd felt that way the first few times leaving Chelsea. Her tears gutted him with guilt. Then he discovered her tears had been more of the crocodile variety.

That adage about the mouse being away and the cat playing had applied. He'd probably never know the full extent of her betrayal. The clandestine meetings and calls.

It sickened him.

She was the last person he wanted to think about while holding Paisley in his arms.

She'd never let him down.

"Your parents seem happy," she said while he swayed her to an admirable cover of Aaron Lewis's version of "What Hurts the Most."

"I'm sure they are." *I used to be.* How twisted was it that in a way, at least where he and Paisley were concerned, he'd been far happier when they were a fake couple. At least then, his life had purpose. Drive.

Give his dad some peace. Practice developing a convincing relationship with Paisley.

Only the joke was on Wayne, because all that work had developed into far more than he'd bargained for. She was a beautiful, smart and funny companion he'd be proud to call his wife. He'd be even prouder for the privilege of calling her son his own. With all of that in mind, what would it take to once and for all exorcise Chelsea from his system? Why couldn't he realize that every day, people all over the world took second chances on love?

If they could do it, why couldn't he?

Maybe he was no longer broken for the simple reason that Paisley's love had miraculously pieced him back together?

Was it possible?

Could boneheaded Logan have been right?

Leaning in, he cocked his head sideways to nuzzle Paisley's neck. The night was warm, and her sweat-dampened skin smelled of lilacs.

"You shouldn't be doing that." She gently pushed him back to a safe distance.

"Why not? Give me a crumb here, babe. I'm trying. Do I have some huge declaration of love all set to go? No. But I'm working on it. We're working on it. I don't know about you, but I think that given the chance, we could lead an amazing life together. Marry me tomorrow. Don't overthink it. Don't stop to obsess over whether it's right or wrong. Let's just do it." He took her hands, raising them to his mouth, kissing her left-hand ring finger. How was it possible he didn't yet know where his team was being shipped, yet already missed her? "Since I bought the companion to your engagement ring, seems like a shame letting it go to waste."

"True, but…" He kissed her quiet. He kissed her soft and slow, parting her lips to sweep her tongue with his. He'd have all the time in the world to figure out what she wanted from him. In the meantime, he refused to let her go. When the song ended, he drew back for air, but not for long. He wanted Paisley to have zero doubt as to the matter of meeting him on that wedding altar.

Which is why his next move was to put her engagement ring back where it belonged—on her finger.

"*If* we do this," she said, eyes shimmering and lips kiss-swollen, while looking at her ring, then back to him, "what are your plans for a wedding license? All we have is the fake."

"Excellent point. There are two ways around this minor issue. One—we wrangle up a local license first thing in the morning. I'll make a few calls. After all, you are marrying a navy SEAL. If I can't pull off such a no-brainer task as getting a wedding license on a Saturday, my CO should strip my Trident."

She rolled her eyes. "What was your second plan?"

"We move forward with our original plan, use the fake, then have a simple civil ceremony back home. Or in Vegas. Wherever you want. No big deal, right?"

"That right there," she said with a poke to his chest, "is why it *is* a big deal. Because I still believe this sudden frenzy to marry has far more to do with fulfilling your dad's dying dream than your own."

Leaving him, Paisley ditched her friend and the remainder of the party in favor of hitching a lonely ride back to the house on a wagon, then retreating to her room and a hot bath.

She wished the long soak made her feel better, but if anything, time alone with her jumbled thoughts only made her more confused.

Did she want to be with Wayne? Of course! But on her terms, which weren't fair to him. As for her irrational fears that she'd be using him in a way similar to what her mom had done with her male targets, Monica was right. Nothing could be further from the truth. But how did Paisley get to the heart of her truth when she'd fallen so hard for Wayne that she could no longer fathom a life without him?

Needing to talk, she dried and dressed and crammed her hair into a messy bun, then padded barefoot through the silent, dark house to his room.

Heart pounding, she found the nerve to knock on his door.

For the longest time, there was no answer. Assuming he was already asleep, she turned to leave, but then he startled her by abruptly opening the door, and she stepped back.

By the light of a dim bedside lamp, she saw him wearing khaki cargo shorts. And nothing else.

"Hey." Paisley gulped. His chiseled abs and chest were the reason for poetry. Pure masculine beauty from which she felt powerless to look away. In the face of her giant baby bump and cankles, his perfection wasn't fair. If they were married for real, she could touch him. All of him. Whenever she wanted. Alas, she'd only signed on for the sham marriage package which made him strictly off-limits.

"What's up?"

"Can I come in?"

"I guess?" He stepped back, waving her inside. "You left the party in an awfully big rush. I figured you'd rather be alone."

"I tried that, but it didn't make me feel much better than when I was with you." While she stood alongside a dresser lined with rodeo memorabilia and sports trophies, trying to focus on anything but his near-nakedness, he closed the door.

"Thanks? I think?" Compared to his apartment, this room was crammed with childhood and teen mementos and color. Rumpled blue bedspread. A blue chair. Big oak desk stacked with books. The walls were lined with photos of Wayne smiling on horseback. Leaping for a football pass. Waving his arms high in victory atop a mountain. In all the years she'd known him, it was odd to just now meet this version. Paisley instantly liked him—except for the shot of him and a pretty teen all dressed up for what a photo stamp labeled Pine Ridge High Prom.

Like her room, his sported a window wall with red curtains closed on the view.

"Sorry about the mess." He stooped to grab a dirty T-shirt and boxers and tossed them both atop his leather satchel. "I wasn't expecting a late-night guest." His slow and sexy grin didn't do much for her resolve to hold tight to her convictions regarding not going through with their wedding.

"Have a seat," He took hold of her arm, guiding her toward the foot of the bed.

"Wayne…"

"Paise…" There he went again with his grin. Would someone kindly remind her why she was here?

She toyed with the tie to her robe, wishing she'd put on more under it than just panties. "I wanted to apologize for what I said at the party. I didn't mean to trivialize our original mission—making your dad's last days better."

"I get it. I asked you to go above and way beyond what you'd originally signed up for, and you're not on board. It's not a problem."

"Yeah, but—"

He pressed his finger over her lips. "There's nothing more to say. Although if you ever do want to marry, I can think of all sorts of pleasant ways you might repay me."

So can I…

She'd forgotten how to breathe.

How to think.

How to do anything other than wish herself free of this increasingly awkward situation. It was wrong to lust for her fake husband. What personal defect had stopped her from finding the real thing? Her very own love. She was beginning to doubt if true love even existed.

"Just kidding. No favors required." He nodded toward the door. "Come on. I'll walk you back to your room."

"Thanks. But first, I have a serious question."

"Shoot."

She forced a breath. "D-do you find me attractive?"

"What?" He coughed. Not a great sign.

"I'm serious. Guys are always drooling over Monica. When I met my baby's father, I thought he was the one, you know? My whole life, I've been alone. It's probably just exhaustion and hormones talking, but sometimes I wonder if I'll ever find the right guy? Do I even want a guy? Would he inevitably be one more person in my life who's destined to let me down?"

"That's a pessimistic attitude." He held out his hands to pull her from the foot of the bed. He was incredibly strong, shouldering not just her physical weight, but emotional whining when he was the one on the verge of losing his father. "Especially, when you have a great offer already on the table from me."

"Thank you. But as great as that offer is, I have to question your sincerity." On her feet with her fingers linked to his, she dared ask, "Why haven't you ever asked me out?"

His smile turned introspective. "Thought about it, but you were intimidating."

"Are you kidding me? Compared to the busty beauties you usually bring home, I'm a wren amongst peacocks."

"If we're talking birds, I'd equate you to a more substantial variety. Maybe a robin? You're solid and smart and dependable. I know you'd call me on my bullshit and never let me put you second to anyone or anything."

"How in the world did you derive all of that from hardly even knowing me beyond friendship."

He shrugged and released her hands. "Gut feel."

"Explain. Because that makes no sense."

"Remember how I told you that by leaving the ranch, I feel like I've let my dad down?"

"Yeah…"

"His expectations for me were unrealistically high. He demanded so much that I wasn't capable of giving."

"But you're a navy SEAL. Aside from being, I don't know, an astronaut or president, isn't that one of the highest achievements a person can attain?"

"Sure, but—" he dropped his gaze "—that's different. It's not personal. I just can't imagine being responsible for another person's heart. I already let my parents down. I could never do that to any woman— especially, not you."

Fair enough. Not the answer she'd expected, but if she hadn't wanted the truth, she shouldn't have asked.

"Taking it a step further, it somehow doesn't matter that Chelsea cheated on me. What matters is that I wasn't man enough for her to want to be faithful. I made lifelong vows that were broken. That makes me a failure."

"Wayne, no…" Her heart ached for this big, strong man whose confidence and emotions had been shredded. "If that's your definition of failure, then I'm far worse off than you. At least you had a commitment. I had a wham-bam, thank you ma'am." She swiped sudden tears.

"Aw, don't say that." He pulled her into his arms and she let him, rejoiced in being held by him. He smoothed his hands up and down her back. "Dr. Dirtbag didn't deserve you. You're amazing."

"I'm not…"

"Yeah, you kind of are." Fingers beneath her chin, he tipped her head back, forcing her gaze to his. "I'm not sure when it happened, but, Paise, I'm crazy about you." With his hands now cupping her cheeks, he hovered his lips dangerously near hers. "Where have you been?"

"Here, all along." *Waiting for you.*

He toyed with her, nipping her bottom lip, caressing her with hints of his warm, yeasty-smelling breath.

She splayed her hands against his chest, boldly exploring his insanely honed pecs while he kissed her neck and jaw and the sensitive hollow at the base of her throat where surely, her pulse beat hard enough for him to see.

Finally, he kissed her lips and she was gone.

Primal urges took hold.

They paused long enough for her to unbutton his fly, freeing him from his boxers. While she worked him, he untied her robe, fingering her through the side of her panties. It had been so long, she came fast and hard, biting her lower lip, crying out in wholly pleasurable pain.

"You okay?" he asked.

"I will be…" Pushing him onto the bed, she slipped off her panties, then, because she couldn't imagine one more moment without having him inside her, she awkwardly joined him on the bed, lowering herself onto him, riding hard until coming again in a glorious technicolor dream.

He stiffened, spilling himself inside her. Her fantasy of him being her baby's father instead of Dr. Dirtbag was now so much more real. As was the fact that she'd just been incredibly irresponsible with her heart.

"That escalated quickly." Wayne brushed the backs of his fingers against her cheek.

"I'm not sure what happened, but I think we can safely say we connect on a physical level."

"No kidding."

"I'm not even sure how to get up—which is almost as mortifying that this happened in the first place."

"How was she supposed to get off of him when he was growing hard again inside her? And it felt amazing?

Now he was the one groaning. "Round two?"

In the dim lamplight, his slow, sexy grin ruled over self-control or sanity.

She leaned down to kiss him.

He rose to return the favor.

He tasted of beer and peach cobbler and the forbidden wonder of the unobtainable. This couldn't happen again. It felt too good. But did he truly love her? He'd said lots of pretty words. But how did she know if he'd meant them? Was she a fool for leaving herself wide open for another potential break?

Her body didn't care.

But she was afraid for her already wary heart.

Chapter Thirteen

"Dad, are you sure you're feeling up to this?" Wayne hated the way his father leaned in his saddle. Used to be he was more comfortable on his horse than the living room sofa.

"Yes, yes. Fresh air best medicine."

Usually, Wayne would have been the first to agree. But after sharing a wild night with Paisley, assuming their wedding was back on, to then wake without her beside him hadn't exactly filled him with warm fuzzies.

He'd been on his way to her room when his dad said they needed to talk—away from the house. Apparently, he had medical papers he wanted Wayne to read.

Combining that emotional knot with the one he already carried for Paisley made for one helluva heavy heart.

The ponderosa pine forest was silent save for the horses' soft footfalls on a thick layer of needles. The smell was incredible. The sight of his father's struggle? Not so much. The ranch grounds had been sun drenched, but the deeper into the valley they rode, the thicker the fog, lending their world an eerie green glow.

"You remember when we come here when you just little boy?"

"Of course. I loved our rides."

"Me, too," his dad said. "We are very blessed. You with beautiful bride and baby. Me, with your m-momma…" The way his voice caught on that last word made Wayne glance over his shoulder to find his strong, proud dad silently crying. It was a sight he'd never witnessed. And it destroyed him.

They rode a half mile deeper into the woods, the whole while with Wayne's stomach churning.

"Dad?" Wayne asked upon entering a glade so dazzlingly green and perfect it could be straight out of a Disney movie.

"Yes, my son?"

"How about we rest here and you show me those papers."

"Yes, yes."

They both dismounted, leaving the horses loose to graze.

In keeping with his old school cowboy demeanor, Wayne's dad wore black chaps over his jeans and his black stallion was named Thunder.

When he noticed his father walking with a limp, Wayne helped him to the flat boulder where they used to bring his mom to picnic when he'd been a kid.

"Thank you," his dad said. "I can manage, but it nice to have my son. I miss you."

"I've missed you, too." Tears clawed the back of his throat. His wasn't ready to say their final goodbye.

"Please take papers from saddlebag. I hide them there from your momma. She big snoop."

"You should tell her."

"I know. But then she cry. I can handle much—but never that. My whole life I fight never to make her cry."

"I know, but this is serious." Wayne approached his father's black stallion, giving his hindquarter a light rub before finding the documents. Lots of them. Crammed haphazardly as if out of sight, out of mind.

Words leaped from the page.

Stage I seminoma.

Treatment plan.

Removal of patient's left testicle.

So many words, but what the hell did any of them mean? Wayne was no doctor. He'd damn near flunked basic field medicine because he couldn't take the sight of blood.

"Dad, do you have testicular cancer?"

His father shook his head. "Too horrible to speak of. They took my manhood. I no longer whole. Humiliating." He broke down in racking sobs that Wayne held him through. "I couldn't tell your momma."

"But, Dad…" Wayne shuffled through more of the documents. "I'm no expert, but look—" He held out a sheet for his father to read. Since he was even worse at reading English than speaking it, Wayne did it for him. "'… Patient's long-term prognosis excellent. Zero cancerous cells detected after testicle removal. Recommended treatment—blood tests for three to six months combined with observation.' Dad, you're not dying, but cured."

"No. I have cancer. All I know with cancer…" He made a slitting motion across his throat. "They die. I die, too. Plus, they took my manhood."

Cautious relief flooded Wayne's system. The air smelled sweeter, the sun shone brighter. Hundreds of pounds had been lifted from his shoulders and all he could think was how excited he was to tell Paisley this whole medical scare had been caused by faulty beliefs and translation.

"Look, I get that your pride has to be hurt, but since you had the surgery, that means they cut the cancer out of you. You don't have it anymore."

"How that possible?" Wayne's father closed his eyes and pressed his hands over his heart. Silvery tears streamed down his leathery cheeks. "I no understand. You get cancer—you die. Everyone know that. Plus, every time I ride, I hurt so bad."

Laughing, Wayne hugged his father. "We've got to get you some English classes. Bottom line, you're going to live for a very long time. But you shouldn't be horseback riding until you're fully healed. That's why you're hurting. Did the doctor give you antibiotics? Pain pills?"

"Yes, but I no take pills. I strong."

"Yes, you are." *And more than a tad bullheaded.* Wayne notched his hat back, drinking in the beauty of this miraculous day. His dad would be fine. His family would remain whole—at least for now.

Only one problem remained—Paisley.

Only she wasn't so much of a problem as she was an enigma. Even after learning his dad would be okay, Wayne still found himself wanting to go ahead with the wedding. But if his dad was no longer sick, what reason did he have? It couldn't be love. Since this was a morning of admissions, okay, he'd fess up. He'd loved Chelsea heart and soul. Once their marriage ended, he'd felt lost. Truth be told, even though Paisley's price for a true marriage was love, Wayne was terrified of the very concept.

He didn't think he was capable of love.

So where did that leave him?

Basically, standing at the altar with no bride.

"GOOD MORNING, SUNSHINE. Happy wedding day!"

"Thank you." Because Paisley was beyond touched by Jules's thoughtful gesture of a second breakfast in bed, she forced a bright smile, praying her soon-to-be mother-in-law wouldn't notice her eyes were swollen and red from crying.

"We have such a busy day. I hate that you and Wayne are bucking the tradition of him seeing his bride before your ceremony, but I understand how it'll be more fun to celebrate together all day. Peter and I once attended a double wedding for identical twins. It was the darnedest thing. They said their vows in unison."

"Fun." The baby kicked hard enough to make Paisley wince.

"Feeling okay? It's perfectly normal if you're having jitters—even second thoughts." Jules fussed with easing the oversize breakfast tray onto the bedside table.

"I'm good." Sort of. But spending the night with Wayne had been a mistake. Now, she had fallen that much deeper with no hope of escaping the depth of her feelings for him. What if she did marry him? Would that make her a horrible person?

How far would Jules's opinion of her plummet were she to learn the truth about Paisley and her son? One issue they had yet to approach was her baby's paternity. Did Wayne ever intend on telling his parents the baby wasn't his? Her eyes stung with pending tears. If only he truly loved her the way Logan loved Monica. The way Peter loved Jules. Then the baby's birth father wouldn't matter, because he would have a new forever daddy in Wayne.

"Oh, honey…" Jules perched beside her on the bed. "What's wrong?"

"Nothing." *Everything.* Did she dare take a deep breath and trust Wayne with her heart? Hours from now, she'd stand at the altar with a man who admittedly didn't love her, but what if he could learn to? Didn't she owe it to herself, to her baby, to at least give him the benefit of the doubt that he was trying? In the same respect, how could she exchange vows with a man who had to *try* loving her? It wasn't fair. Love was supposed to be easy. Paisley swiped hormonal tears with the back of her hands. "Thank you."

"It's just breakfast."

"No—I mean for making me feel so welcome in your home. I've never had a real home. My mother and I moved a lot and to think that my son will grow up being part of all of this…" Paisley forced a deep breath. "It's overwhelming. But good."

"Aw, you are such a precious girl. Our son is lucky to have found you. Each time you see him, even when you think no one is watching, your expression brightens with the radiance of when the sun punches through clouds after a storm. Sheer poetry. I never saw that with Wayne's first wife. You, my sweet girl, will be his last wife. The woman with whom my son grows old. As his mother, you have no idea what a comfort that is."

Cue more tears.

Whatever doubts Paisley had about going through with the ceremony were banished. For Jules, maybe even selfishly for herself, Paisley would marry Wayne with their fake license. When they returned to San Diego she would make it official. With him by her side, she would have her baby and, God willing, she'd never be without a family again.

Jules drew her into a wonderful hug. The kind of hug Paisley had craved as a little girl. Now that she was a woman on the verge of becoming a mother, never had she needed this kind of support more.

"Tell me about your family," Jules said.

"I'm an orphan." Another lie. They were stacking up, waiting to topple, smothering her beneath their weight. But Paisley was strong. If there was nothing else her mom had taught her, it was to persevere under pressure.

Not until this very moment, sharing this special time with her new mother, did Paisley realize how very much she needed all of this to work. If it didn't, there was no safety net.

Only a lifetime of regrets for things she might have done differently.

WAYNE LED HIS dad on a gentler route back to the barn, then insisted his father grab a nap while Wayne cared for the horses.

It had been an amazing morning.

Part of him couldn't wait to share it with Paisley. Another part of him worried he shouldn't. If she knew his dad was no longer in crisis mode, would she bolt? He didn't want to lie to her. In the same breath, he didn't want to lose her. She might have said she was ultimately on the hunt for love, but that was a far cry from her admitting she loved him.

They'd been so hot together, but there was a lot more to marriage than sex. But since they were already friends, wasn't that a head start?

Finished in the barn, he found her surrounded by a gaggle of women Monica's dad had flown in for the occasion. They'd all converged on the barn's loft apartment. Their laughter and Brad Paisley's crooning had drifted to him in the stalls.

There was such a commotion of hair drying and makeup that no one heard him come up the stairs.

He saw her before she caught sight of him.

She sat in a rocker with her feet up on a padded floral ottoman. Monica must've have pulled off the impossible by finding a white maternity jogging suit with Bride monogrammed in hot pink script. Monica wore a matching one in a considerably smaller version.

Paisley looked beautiful—her makeup had been done and her hair expertly styled, but her expression was sad. Wistful. She sat alone, nursing a steaming mug of what he guessed was herbal tea. The look she cast her best friend held a longing that cut deep. Monica was all smiles, laughing and taking selfies with her friends. She was secure in her adoration for Logan and his unshakable love for her.

How many times had Paisley admitted to wanting the same? It crushed him that he still wasn't prepared to give it and wasn't sure when—if ever—he would. The only thing he did know was that he couldn't let her go.

As if she'd felt his stare from across the room, she looked up. Their gazes locked.

He found a smile. Waved.

She did the same.

He entered the vast, vaulted-ceilinged room, sticking to the perimeter to draw the least amount of attention. He reached Paisley, then held out his hand. "Want to find someplace a little more quiet to talk?"

"We probably should."

He helped her from the chair, out of the room and down the stairs. His pulse raced not from exertion, but nerves. He owed it to her to tell her the truth about his dad. In the same respect, if there wasn't going to be a wedding, he owed it to his folks to break the news to them now.

He walked Paisley to the house's center courtyard and eased her onto a bench that faced the gurgling three-tier fountain.

"You left early this morning," he said by way of an icebreaker. "I was hoping for at least a good-morning kiss."

Her cheeks reddened adorably. "Last night got a little out of control."

"Am I complaining?"

"No, but…" She looked up and when their gazes met,

he lost all sense of time and place. All that mattered was now, and getting her to understand his point of view. "I just never expected us to go that far."

"If it's not a problem for you, it sure as hell isn't for me." He took her hand, easing his fingers between hers. "I got some great news."

"What's up? Is it about your dad?" She angled closer to face him. Their knees touched. Such a simple gesture, yet it struck him as intimate. Every time they touched had become a special occasion.

Caught off guard by the emotions blocking his throat, he nodded. "I was on my way to see you earlier, but Dad drew me aside. He wanted me to go over his medical paperwork, so we saddled the horses and hit the trail."

"What did you find out?"

"Amazing news." He slowly exhaled. "He does have cancer, but it's testicular. His doctor caught it early enough to be reasonably sure it won't come back. But my dad's English is so poor, all he heard was 'cancer' and he flipped out, assuming it meant instant death. Of course, he was mortified to have lost a part of his manhood, but if I can keep him off his horse long enough to heal, he should be fine."

"Wayne, that's incredible!" She tossed her arms around him for a fierce hug. "That's the best news ever. You must be thrilled."

"I am. I really am." His smile faded. "Only there's one issue needing to be resolved."

"Our wedding?" Head bowed, she said, "I guess there's no need to go through with it, huh?"

"Here's the thing…" He cupped his hand to her cheek, brushing her lower lip with his thumb. "Paise, I want to marry you. I want to help raise your baby boy. The time we've spent together has been great. I've always thought you were a great friend and neighbor, but now…" Leaning in to kiss her, he tasted salty tears that had streamed onto her lips. It reminded him of his father's speech, about how he hated seeing his mother cry. Wayne now experienced that same ache. "Don't cry, angel. Like I said last night at the barbecue, let's not overanalyze this. Let's just do it. With my dad's long-term prognosis excellent, it makes sense. Why shouldn't we be a happy family?"

"Because we're not in love."

"With a friendship as solid as ours, we don't have to be. Your whole concept of love is an issue of semantics. I'm sure a boatload of solid marriages have been forged on foundations of a lot less."

"Yeah, like yours to Chelsea? Look how that turned out."

His hopeful smile faded. "Leave her out of this. I need an answer, Paise. Is this wedding a go, or should I tell my folks we're done?"

She took a lifetime to shake her head, then whispered, "I'll marry you."

Chapter Fourteen

Safely ensconced in Monica's bridal suite, surrounded by all the trappings of the quintessential wedding celebration—champagne and iced white cookies and cupcakes. Laughter and giggles. Yards of satin and tulle. Paisley should have been happy. This was her wedding day. For real. It represented the sum of her every wish come true—all save for one.

Love.

Wayne had delivered a highly convincing speech. So much so that she almost believed if he didn't love her now, that he could grow to love her in their shared future. But was that enough? Or was she being greedy to even expect perfection?

"Why so glum?" Monica asked. She held a champagne flute filled with sparkling cider in one hand and her phone in the other—no doubt in the event a photo-op presented itself for her social media empire. In case her mother called, Paisley had left her cell back in her room. The last thing she needed on this already emotionally charged day was a blast from her past in the form of a reunion with her absentee mom.

"I don't know." Truly she didn't. Paisley rubbed her baby. "I should be blissfully happy, right? I've got a great guy willing to marry me and be a father to my baby boy. I should be dancing like your grandma Lucy."

"She does have some moves." Both women looked to the senior citizen shaking her tail feathers to DNCE's "Cake by the Ocean."

"Seriously, Mon, what's wrong with me?"

"Nothing." She wrapped Paisley in a great hug. "I think maybe your head hasn't quite caught up with your heart."

"What's that mean?" Paisley wrinkled her nose.

"Deny it all you want, but you and I both know you've crushed on Wayne forever."

Heat rising on her cheeks, Paisley didn't try hiding her smile. "Guilty."

"Okay, so all this time you two have been faking having the hots for each other, just reinforced your genuine hots for the guy. And now you get to be with him forever. But it happened so fast, you need a minute to get used to the idea. But that's good, too, because now you have a lifetime to spend together. Makes perfect sense, right?"

"I love you." Paisley gave her friend another hug. "In a crazy Monica way, that does compute. But you have to know, he still hasn't said he loves me. What if he never does?"

"So what? It's just a word, Paise. If you want to dissect something, look deeper into the man's actions. He can't keep his hands off you. He's probably going to be awesome in bed. He might even— Oh, you naughty girl!"

Paisley's cheeks practically caught fire.

At the mention of bed, her mind ventured straight to the memories of her and Wayne's wild night. Good grief… If there was ever a motivation to stay with a guy, the tricks he did with his hands should have been all the encouragement she needed.

"You and Wayne left the barbecue early to do the deed, didn't you?"

"It wasn't exactly like that, but let's just say we may have consummated our relationship earlier than the honeymoon."

"Was it amazing?"

"I'm not telling you!" Paisley hid her grin behind the napkin she'd used for her cookie.

"I'll take that as a yes." She clapped and smiled. "This makes me so happy. I love that my best friend is finally getting a great guy."

"Wait—" Paisley held up her hands. "Did you actually refer to Wayne as a great guy? Do I need to check you for a fever? I thought you two were sworn enemies?"

Monica laughed. "Ever since he showed us that awesome thrift store, I might have decided to give him a second chance."

Paisley felt the same. Only her second chance for Wayne hadn't been found through shopping, but adoring. She really did have all the right happy, giddy tingles for Wayne.

But did he have the same for her?

"You look incredible," Wayne said to Paisley beneath the ivy-covered pergola in his mother's garden. The rest of the wedding party finished lunch beside the pool. A trio of harpists provided ethereal mood music. The ceremonies weren't until tonight, but Monica had packed every second of their big day with activities. If she asked him one more time to pose for her Instagram, he'd chuck her phone in the pool's deep end. "Thanks again for agreeing to marry me."

"Don't." She sat on a padded iron bench beside a trickling fountain.

"Compliment your dress?"

"Patronize me. And for the record, my wedding dress is beautiful. This makes me look like a walking tent, but it was the only thing in my closet that fit." She fingered the pale green silky fabric. Didn't she realize it matched her stunning pistachio eyes?

"How am I patronizing you when I realize you have reservations about taking vows?"

She sighed, arching her head back while closing her eyes. "We're talking in circles and I'm sick of it. If I had my way, we'd get married right now, then head back to San Diego. Every time I see your mom tearing up while snapping pics of us, I want to hurl."

"You've got a beef with my mom?"

"No. I love her, which is why I feel horrible lying to her. After the baby is born, have you thought about what happens next? Will you formally adopt him?"

"If that's what you want. Is it?"

Worrying her lower lip, she nodded. "I don't ever want him feeling alone or unloved."

"Hey…" He planted his hand beneath her chin, urging her to meet his view. "Is that how you grew up?"

She nodded.

"I know your dad died, but where's your mom now?"

"I'm too ashamed to tell you."

"Try me. Or have you already forgotten my dad's recent near-death experience?"

"How could I forget?" she said with a faint smile. "Best relationship incubation service around. Monica should find a way to duplicate his technique for a new dating app. With her love for all things social media, she'd make a fortune."

"Funny. But, babe," he said, taking her hands and giving them a light squeeze, "what's up with your mom? You say you want a family, but if she's alive out there somewhere, why isn't she here now?"

"For all I know, she could be on her way. It's been a year since we last spoke. Before that, she was in a Florida prison for bilking a retiree out of his fortune. I'm not clear on the details, but her actions make me sick. She's a user in the worst possible sense of the word."

"It all becomes clear." Wayne stroked her palms. "You don't want to be guilty of using me or my family?"

She shook her head, sniffing back fresh tears. "I had no idea your family ranch is more of an empire."

"How could you? And who cares? Maybe one day we'll end up here? Maybe we won't? Regardless, I want to be with you. Is that love? I have no idea. But for now, it feels damned good."

"For now." She turned to him. "But what if a few months or years from now, you feel trapped?"

"I could turn that around on you. What if you get tired of me being a slob or missing birthdays and anniversaries and holidays because of surprise deployments?" *Like the one I learned about just last night?* "All this time, you've presumed I'm the one holding the power, when all along it's been you, Paisley." He cupped her cheek, brushing the pad of his thumb along her full lower lip. "One of your biggest charms is that you have no idea what a huge catch you are."

"Keyword *huge*." She rubbed her enormous belly.

"Don't do that. You asked me not to patronize you—fine. But only if you agree to knock it off with the self-deprecating humor. You are carrying a baby. That's a miracle. You're adorable and smart as a whip and never back down. You make me laugh and watch movies I know I'll hate, but you somehow know me so well that I end up thoroughly enjoying every minute of them. Kind of like every time I'm with you. God's honest truth? I can't wait to marry you. To spend the rest of my life coaxing as many smiles out of those gorgeous lips as I possibly can."

Was it possible to be high on the potent drug of kind words? If so, Paisley never wanted to come down.

When Wayne leaned in for a kiss, she met him halfway.

For an eternity, they searched each other's gazes, the universes still waiting to be discovered within. Was this love? Who knew? Who cared? The champagne bubbles making her giddy from fingers to toes said she no longer needed that label.

Once Wayne pressed his lips to hers, all she needed was him. His gentle pressure, the tease of his tongue, the nip at her lower lip and exchange of breaths and souls. This was all too perfect to be real, but here she was and here Wayne was and no matter what, she was never going back. She was never giving up the family she'd searched her whole life to find.

A squeal came from beyond their ivy-covered hideaway, then a splash.

"Logan, noooooo!" Monica?

Paisley frowned. "This can't be good."

"Come on." Wayne stood, then grabbed both her hands to help steady her on her feet. "Let's see what's going on."

By the time they rejoined the party, bedlam had broken loose. The harpists had been replaced by a boom box and Luke Bryan crooning for his "country girl" to "shake it for me."

"What did we miss?" Wayne asked.

"At least a few dozen glasses." Paisley pointed toward the half-dozen empty champagne bottles on most tables.

Guests who weren't in the pool danced alongside it, laughing and clapping and helping themselves to more lobster and champagne and crazy fun in the sun.

"Now, this is a great wedding." Wayne had already removed his tie, and now worked on his jacket, dropping both to the terra-cotta pool deck. He eyed her. "Are you going in voluntarily or am I going to have to coerce you?"

"Oh no." She backed away, shaking her head. "Don't even think about it."

His devilish grin said he wasn't only thinking about it, but already lunging for her, scooping her into his arms.

Clinging to him, closing her eyes in anticipation of an ungainly splash, he thrilled her by easing into bathtub-warm turquoise water. The sensation of weightlessness prompted a groan of sheer bliss.

"Feel good?"

"Better."

"Better than sex?"

She peeked around him to ensure his mom or any of the other guests hadn't overheard. "The only thing better than this would be sex while in the pool."

"That can be arranged."

She giggled. "Tonight, Mr. Brustanovitch, I might just take you up on that offer."

"In that case, almost Mrs. Brustanovitch..." he kissed her nice and slow "...I'm thinking I should track down the pastor so we can get this show on the road."

"You and Paisley looked awfully cozy in the pool," Logan said while checking the collar of his white button-down in the hall bathroom mirror. After the impromptu pool party, as more guests streamed onto the property, Monica's appalled wedding planner shooed both brides and grooms to their respective corners of the ranch. "I assume that means you worked everything out?"

"I really think we did." Wayne added his black sports

coat over his white shirt, thrilled that the women had picked jeans, cowboy boots, hats and no bow ties to finish out the men's wedding attire. "Thanks for last night's advice, man. I don't mean to jinx us, but I think we might have a shot at this marriage thing."

"I'm happy for you. For us. I feel the same about Monica."

"Have you heard from any of the guys?"

"Monk texted. They're finding the assigned mission a bit more taxing than anticipated, but I'm sure they'll get it done."

"Who all's with him?"

"Lion, Jeb and Houston. They took the wrong exit off I-10."

"And we regularly trust them with our lives?"

Logan laughed. "Did you and Paisley have the talk about next week's deployment?"

"That would be a negative. Thought we agreed to keep it on the DL."

"I think that's best. I'd be lying, though, if I said I wasn't dreading leaving. Did Paisley tell you Monica's pregnant?"

"No way? Congratulations, man."

"Thanks."

"Did this have anything to do with the speedy wedding?"

"Nah. She's not very far along. We just found out last week—haven't even told our parents. Guess this is all so new and unexpected we're afraid to jinx it. The speed of our wedding had more to do with the fact that we've both dallied at this for years. When she told me it made her feel like I didn't appreciate her by not putting a ring on it, something deep down snapped. She turns me to mush inside, man. It's the damnedest thing."

Wayne was unfortunately growing all too familiar with the mush sensation. Would it go away the longer he and Paisley were together? Or only get worse?

"Nervous?" Paisley asked Monica a few minutes before walking down the aisle. With her hair swept high into an elegant looping updo, and her strapless, beaded gown clinging to her curves, Paisley couldn't decide if her friend looked more like a Roman goddess or modern-day royalty. Either way, she was stunning. Her brilliant smile proved her best accessory.

Monica squeezed her hand. "Not with you beside me. I love that we're walking down the aisle together, then sharing my father once we reach the altar."

"Me, too. I love him almost as much as you."

Paisley struggled to hold back her tears as she hugged her longtime friend.

Gathering her composure, Paisley tried to squelch her apprehension. At least for once, with the help of Monica's hairstylist and makeup artist, she felt beautiful. She'd forgotten how perfectly her dress fit, and fell in love with it all over again from the rhinestone belt that rode atop her baby bump to the bodice hugging her breasts in all the right places. She couldn't have been more thrilled with it. The long satin skirt with its train made her feel as if she wouldn't be walking down the aisle, but floating.

She'd opted to wear her hair down in spiraling curls

held back with an elegant crystal clip. Jules let Paisley borrow her wedding pearls. Her garter was blue, her dress was vintage—a nicer word for something old—and her something new was the pearl bracelet Monica had given her before lunch.

"Ready?" Monica asked.

Paisley nodded. "I really am. Never in a million years would I have predicted how this would all turn out."

"You deserve to be happy, Paise. You and your baby boy."

"Aw, you, too." Laughing, crying, they exchanged hugs as the wedding planner shooed them down the aisle.

The Brustanovitch family barn had been constructed during the gold rush of 1863 and lovingly restored through the years, but today, with the rafters festooned with thousands of white roses and ivy, with Ball jar candles hanging at intermittent heights in between, it looked like she and Monica were stepping into a fairy tale. The smell was equally as sweet as the anticipation fluttering in Paisley's stomach.

A hundred guests, who had been sitting on white-blanket-covered hay bales, now stood when a trio of mandolins played the "Wedding March."

"Smile!" the wedding planner coached from behind them.

Paisley didn't need encouraging. Her cheeks hurt from the size of her grin.

The walk down the aisle took ages, but upon reaching the flower-adorned gazebo Monica's planner had a crew construct for them to use as an altar, Paisley had eyes only for Wayne. Never had she seen him look more handsome in his crisp white shirt and sports coat. Jeans that hugged his powerful thighs, along with his sexy black cowboy boots and hat.

Had there ever been a luckier bride?

Upon reaching the altar, Monica's dad, Conrad, escorted them both up the low stairs to present them to their grooms, then formally gave them to the new men in their lives. Conrad's kindness might seem like a small thing to some, but to Paisley, having grown up with no father, it meant the world.

Finally, she stood next to Wayne.

He towered over her, performing the impossible and making her feel petite and protected and cherished.

While the pastor said something to Logan and Monica, Wayne leaned close, whispering, "Surprise, gorgeous. This is the real deal."

"What do you mean?"

"Our vows, the ceremony, it's all real. My team pulled off the impossible by getting us a legit Arizona license."

"What about my signature?"

"I've got a guy for that. Best damned forger in the navy." Wayne winked.

Paisley's mind was spinning. Her pulse racing. *What?* Hadn't they agreed to be done with lies? She thought they'd have a legal ceremony back in San Diego.

"Did you hear me, babe?" While Logan and Monica took solemn oaths to love and protect each other for the rest of their lives, Wayne was still boasting about what a stellar job his friend had done with the forged document. "We pulled it off. Isn't this great? Exactly what you wanted."

No. No, this was nothing like she wanted. She wanted a simple "I love you." Not yet another *fake* anything. She wanted to make Jules and Peter proud of her. She wanted to be the kind of wife and mother who could be proud of herself.

A guest on the front row could be heard softly crying. The woman in the lavender suit blotted a tissue to her eyes, making her unrecognizable until she lowered it. And smiled. Moving just her fingers in a tight wave.

No, no, no… A sharp ringing blocked the pastor's voice from reaching Paisley's ears. *This isn't possible. I'm hallucinating.*

"Babe?" She saw Wayne's lips move, but couldn't be sure what he'd said.

Why wouldn't the room stop spinning?

Paisley didn't have time to ponder the question when her every instinct told her to *run*.

Chapter Fifteen

"Paise? Babe, what's the matter?" As soon as he'd spotted her unsteady stance and out-of-focus gaze, Wayne knew she was in trouble. He'd seen enough guys faint from heat stroke to recognize the signs. But then she hadn't gone down as expected, but taken off, running as fast as a seriously pregnant woman could away from him and their shocked guests.

Attendees at first shared a near-collective gasp, and then chaos ruled when Wayne also charged down the wrong end of the aisle.

"What the hell?" he asked after chasing his bride damn near to the house. He grabbed her upper arm, tugging her around to face him.

"I—I can't do this." She shook her head, then scanned the crowd emerging from the barn. "I'm sorry. I thought I could, but then I—I saw my mom and panicked."

"What the hell does your mom have to do with leaving me at the altar? I feel like an idiot, Paise. How could you do this in front of not only all my friends, but Mom and Dad. Our whole reason for marrying was for him."

"Exactly. Our wedding should be about us. But it doesn't matter. I'm sorry I hurt you, but what's done is done. I can't take it back, and— Great…"

Wayne followed Paisley's stare.

A woman approached. She was petite with stylish red hair the same shade as Paisley's and a light purple dress that matched her purse and shoes.

Upon seeing her, Paisley shook her head, calling, "Go away! You shouldn't be here."

"I am here."

"I don't want you to be," Paisley whispered.

"Tough." Arms crossed, the woman Wayne assumed was Paisley's mother showed no sign of budging.

But then Monica joined the party. Followed by Logan and Wayne's parents and more people he didn't want to see. Hadn't he already been humiliated enough? Did they need an up close and personal view of his pain? Make no mistake—he was hurting. It wasn't until Paisley ran out on him that he'd realized just how much he needed her.

"What's wrong?" Monica brushed Wayne aside, feeling Paisley's forehead. "You might have a fever. I know this look. Were you afraid of tossing your cookies in the middle of our vows? Is that why you left?"

Paisley nodded.

Wayne wanted to call her out on the lie, but her friend's version of events was far more palatable than reality.

"Poor thing." Jules rubbed Paisley's back. "Let's get you inside and resting."

"Thank you," Paisley said, "but please don't fuss.

I'm fine. All I want is for Monica and Logan to finish their vows. Please don't let me ruin your special day."

"Sweetie," Monica said, "this is *our* special day. I love you. I want us all to take our vows together."

"I know." Paisley wrapped her friend in a hug, whispering for only her to hear, "Please go get married. This is complicated."

"But…" Monica pulled back to wipe Paisley's tears with the embroidered wedding hanky her father had given her. "Okay. You take care of you. I'll cover."

"Thanks. I'm so sorry. And seriously, please squeeze every ounce of joy from the rest of your day."

Now Monica had also grown teary, but she nodded.

"Come on, everyone!" She began wrangling guests back to the barn to witness her and Logan's ceremony. "Sadly, my fellow bride is suffering from round-the-clock morning sickness, so while she rests up for the reception, I've got a man to lasso."

Laughter at least lightened the mood for their guests, but Paisley felt anger radiating from Wayne as he led her from the yard to her guest room.

Unfortunately, Jules followed.

Thankfully, Paisley's mother had not.

"Just as soon as you feel able," Jules said, fussing with getting Paisley into bed, then taking off her shoes and adjusting pillows behind her head, "I'll have the pastor come up here. You two should be official in no time."

"Thank you, Jules. But I'm sorry. For Wayne and me, there isn't going to be a wedding." She wiped fresh tears, hating the hormonal rush keeping her in a perpetually teary condition. "I thought I could keep up this lie, but I can't. Not anymore."

Jules said, "Honey, you're exhausted. I'm sure you'll feel differently come morning. I'm not sure what you mean about lying, but I refuse to accept the fact that you don't love my son."

"O-of course, I do." Paisley covered her nose with Monica's handkerchief. "But I don't think my love is enough."

"This is BS." Wayne slapped the palm of his hand against the nearest wall. "Mom, please leave us alone."

"I don't think that's a good idea." Jules looked from her son to Paisley. "You two might need a referee. At the very least, a voice of reason."

"Please," Paisley said. "It probably is best if we're alone."

"For the record, I disagree." Jules kissed and hugged them both before leaving, closing the door behind her.

Alone with Wayne, the walls closed around her, making the room feel perilously small. Where had all the oxygen gone?

"Don't do this." Wayne raked his hands through his hair. "Don't you dare do this when we've come so far."

"Have we? Really? What's wrong with you? Bragging about having forged my name on a marriage license when you should have been focused mind, body and soul on vows we were making to each other for the rest of our lives. Instead, you were thrilled about having duped not only your parents, but the system."

"Don't you dare pin this all on me. I was psyched because having the official document meant we would be legally man and wife. I thought that's what you wanted? Hell—back in San Diego, you were the one who first suggested using a fake license to get through today's ceremony."

"That was back when we thought your dad was dying. But now we know he's not, and that changes everything. You don't know what I truly want, Wayne. You never did. But you're right. I'm just as much at fault for ever agreeing to all this scheming in the first place. From day one, it was wrong and deep down, I think we both knew it."

"Bullshit." He sat beside her, taking her hand, stroking it as if she were a doll or beloved pet. "What difference does it make how we got together? All that matters is that we are together. Period. End of story."

"This—today—was supposed to have been our beginning."

"Swear to God, Paisley, if you say this is the end, you might as well be dead to me. I'm not playing games." He dropped her hand as if she'd burned him.

"You think this is a game to me? I feel so serious in my convictions that a marriage should be based upon love and not lies, that seeing my lying, ex-convict of a mother nearly caused me to black out. Trust me, no one realizes more than me what's at stake."

"Let's talk about your mom. What was she doing here?"

"I don't have a clue. Monica's constantly posting her location on Instagram. Could be my mother follows the store, follows Monica and me, and decided now was the perfect time for a family reunion. She calls all the time. Maybe she thought this was a foolproof way to make me see her."

"Why wouldn't you see her? She's your mom—not a monster."

"Maybe to me, she's my only monster? When I saw her, it reminded me how much of her life—her relationship with men—had been based on lies. Knowing that, I couldn't stand there in front of God and your parents doing the same thing."

"That's freakin' great." He raised his hands, only to slap them against his thighs. "I'm now being judged based on the sins of a woman I've never met. Thanks for the vote of confidence."

"It's more complicated than that. You could never understand." For the last time, she removed her engagement ring and handed it to him.

"You're right, Paise." He squeezed his hand holding the ring into a tight fist. "I can't understand how you claim to love me, yet keep dicking me around. Even Chelsea wasn't this cruel. When it was over, she cut me off cold. One day she was with me, the next she wasn't. But you're all over the map."

"You think you're not? You're the king of mixed messages. But it doesn't matter. None of this crap matters because we're not getting married—*ever*. We let one lone night of great sex and the romance of what Monica and Logan share go to our heads. We wanted to make your father happy, but did we ever once stop to consider what makes us happy?"

"You." Wayne didn't bother hiding his tears. "You and your baby were what made me happy. Now? Con-

grats. You get your way, Paise. I no longer give a shit."
He stormed away, but then turned back for one, last
scathing look. "For the record, you promised you'd
never leave me. That you'd always be with me. You
weren't the type of girl who leaves her friends when
they need her. Ha. Way to go on making good on all of
your perfectly empty words."

When Wayne left the room, closing the door behind
him, only then did Paisley allow herself to break down.
Damn her mother. Of all days, why had she chosen now
to reinsert herself into her daughter's life?

Don't do that, her conscience warned.

*Don't blame your mom for your own fears and in-
securities. The real problem here is you. Your inabil-
ity to love yourself has rendered you incapable of fully
loving anyone else.*

If she did love Wayne with all her heart, one more
little white lie between them would have been no big
deal. It would have been something to laugh about over
dinner parties when they'd grown old.

But from a young impressionable age, no matter how
desperately Paisley had wanted her fairy-tale ending,
she'd been taught by the master that for women like
her, fairy tales never came true.

BECAUSE SHE WAS too emotionally and physically exhausted to make the long return trek to San Diego that
evening, Paisley accepted Jules and Peter's kind offer
to stay the night. In the morning, Conrad offered to fly
her home in his jet, and she'd accepted.

You're dead to me.

Wayne's words had been unspeakably cruel. He'd crossed a line from which they could never come back. She knew him well enough to understand that had been his pain talking and not him. But years from now, when he found the right woman, he'd be grateful to Paisley for letting him go.

He didn't love her. He felt obligated to her.

He had enough of his father's Russian pride to never allow himself to back down from a challenge. That's all she'd been.

Judging by the confusion raging in her own heart, her feelings for him couldn't have amounted to much more.

By morning, the gloomy weather outside her room's picture window reflected her mood. Paisley showered and dressed in maternity jeans and a pale pink sweater, struggling with her socks and sneakers. She left her boots and cowboy hat in the guest room's closet. It would hurt too much to have them staring at her back in San Diego.

She pulled her hair back into a ponytail, opted to skip makeup, then set off in search of the people she'd hurt.

Hoping to find Jules in the kitchen, Paisley was surprised to see Peter instead. He hummed a nonsensical tune while loading the tray Jules had used the past two days to bring her breakfast in bed.

"Good morning," Paisley said.

Peter clamped his hand to his chest. "You gave me start."

"I'm sorry."

"No. Is good. We need talk. I want you marry my boy, yes?"

With her perpetual waterworks threatening to fall, Paisley shook her head.

"But baby need daddy." He took the liberty of patting her bump. She didn't mind. If anything, it came as a relief to learn Wayne's parents were still speaking to her. "Our grandson need his father."

"Remember, hon?" Jules entered the kitchen behind Paisley. "Wayne talked to us about this. Paisley's baby isn't his biological son."

"Eh…" Peter waved off her words. "Make no difference to me. Baby is baby. We love it the same."

"When did Wayne tell you the truth?" Paisley asked, hugging herself.

"Yesterday. Before the wedding. Peter confessed, as well. I'm beyond relieved that he'll be okay, but furious with him for keeping his cancer from me. All that aside, if that's why you broke things off—because of all these secrets and lies—Paisley, we don't think less of you or in any way hold you responsible. That said, what you and Wayne share is real. You can't deny having strong affection for my son."

Paisley bowed her head.

"If you tell me you feel nothing for him, I'll back off, but until then, Peter and I still choose you to be our daughter-in-law."

"You guys…" Paisley drew them both into a group hug. "You are both so dear. More than anything, I wish things could be different."

"Then make them different," Jules said. "Wayne

tried explaining what little he knew about your past. For what it's worth, your mother introduced herself to us last night, then peaceably left. She seemed lovely."

It's an act. She's poison inside. Just like me.

Paisley shook her head. "I'm sorry. I can't do this. Where's Wayne? I need to say goodbye."

"Oh, honey, you didn't hear?"

"Apparently not." *What now?* What else could possibly happen to make this situation worse?

"Wayne and his entire team were called out on an emergency deployment. They weren't supposed to have left till next week, but I guess the matter escalated and they had to go early. We said our goodbyes at 4:00 a.m. Monica was so upset."

"*Oh no…*" Paisley's knees threatened to buckle. She grabbed hold of the granite counter's edge for support.

"Stay with us until Wayne comes home." Jules wrapped her arm around Paisley's waist. "We'll get you set up with a great local doctor, establish a birthing plan. I'll be your Lamaze coach."

"Jules, Peter, how can I thank you?" Paisley hugged them again. This time, fiercely. Would she see them again? Odds were, she would not.

And if Wayne was to get injured while he was overseas?

Her heart thundered at the mere thought.

If Wayne were to be injured because her signature brand of crazy had served as a contagion, Paisley would never forgive herself.

Chapter Sixteen

"You can't avoid her forever," Monica said in Paisley's office. With her due date only a week away, Paisley was tying up loose ends on the last of her open design projects. As for the open wound in her heart ever since her split with Wayne? She doubted that would ever be healed.

"I can and will avoid my mother till the end of time." Paisley rifled through the various layers of samples and client folders littering her normally tidy desk. "Have you seen the Levys' master bath marble sample? Since they added to their project, I promised bookended slabs for their shower wall but—"

Monica sipped from a ginger ale. With her morning sickness in full swing, the two of them made quite a pair. "I wasn't going to say anything, but your mom approached me at the reception. She told me she learned about our weddings through my Instagram. She explained how many times she's called you, but you never answer. I felt horrible, standing there, acting like this was news to me when I know how many times you ignored her calls. I'm sorry, okay? It's my fault she was there. But you get all the blame for giving her the cold shoulder."

"There's no blame. Only work. Lots and lots of work that has to get done before my little angel makes his appearance."

Monica collapsed onto the sofa. "I feel like dog doo. Have you felt this lousy for the last nine months?"

"Pretty much."

"Fantastic." Monica groaned. "Did you ever stop to think your mom might share insight that could help you repair the damage of leaving Wayne at the altar?"

"It wasn't that dramatic. I might have bolted in front of everyone, but for all they know, I was sick. I broke up with him in private."

From her reclining position, Monica snorted. "Like that makes it so much better? Logan and the rest of the guys knew the score. Poor Wayne was crushed. I'm not saying you should have gone through with the wedding if you weren't feeling it, but there had to be an easier way to let him down? Talk to your mom, Paise. You owe me that much for nearly giving me a heart attack in the middle of my wedding."

"Stop. You're clearly fine. And anyway, it's not like I planned it."

"Please call. I got an email from Logan last night, and he's guessing the team will be back on US soil in a few weeks. That gives you plenty of time to figure out your feelings, have your baby, then go with me to the base to welcome home our guys."

Paisley leaned forward, resting her forehead against

the Levys' cool, calming marble sample. "I don't have a guy."

"Of course, you do."

"Wayne said he's done with me."

"He's not allowed to make that decision until you've officially declared yourself done with him."

"Isn't that what I did by walking out on our wedding and returning his ring?" The events of that night seemed blurry. Only the pain was still sharp. After the fact, holding on to the strict moral code that had kept her sane in the face of her mother's prison sentence no longer seemed as urgent.

Was Monica right? Could Paisley benefit from a long talk with her mom?

There was only one way to find out...

"INCOMING!" LOGAN SHOUTED at the first concussive thump and then squeal of an approaching missile.

Wayne rounded the corner of a cinder block wall about three seconds shy of having his leg blown off. That was too close. "You okay?"

"Just dandy." Logan took Monica's photo from the thigh pocket on his cargo pants, giving it a quick kiss before checking the ammo remaining in his SCAR-L assault rifle.

"Glad you're keeping your head in the game." Wayne was too proud to admit it, but he missed Paisley. How was she feeling? Had she delivered her baby? He felt like shit about not being there for her—even if she didn't want him for her husband, he would always be there as her friend. They'd both exchanged harsh words the night that was supposed to have been the happiest of their lives.

If something happened to him over here and he didn't get a chance to apologize…

Well, let's hope it didn't come to that.

"Ready to clear the next floor?"

"Yeah. Let's do it."

For an intense twenty-three minutes, Wayne and Logan searched the abandoned apartment building where a terrorist cell had holed up.

Pop, pop, pop!

Wayne answered the gunfire with rounds of his own.

The rest of the team worked up and down the block of the formerly thriving Somalian town. Decades of fighting had turned it into a series of architectural skeletons whose steel bones were tragically exposed.

For an instant, he closed his eyes.

He saw Paisley hugging her baby bump back on the ranch, standing at the yard's edge, backlit by a bragging sky.

Pop, pop. Pop, pop, pop!

Boom!

The firefight lasted another thirty minutes until their team sniper signaled the enemy rooftop shooters had been cleared. All well and good for the moment, but these terrorist cells were like persistent roaches. Exterminate twenty, yet there always seemed to be a hundred more.

While his primary thoughts were always on protecting his team, in the background, Paisley was there. Her shy smile and coppery hair glinting in the ranch's

Arizona sun. He loved his job, but in that instant, he couldn't help but wonder if he maybe loved her more? His family ranch more? Could he be content living out the rest of his days helping his father with the cattle breeding and his mom with her baking? Most of all, could he be the kind of husband to Paisley and father to her son that they both deserved?

"I REPEATEDLY CALLED, but you ignored me. I'm sorry I showed up at your wedding uninvited. I thought it might be a nice gesture. That maybe you deserved a more personal approach." Paisley's mother fingered her white cloth napkin's rolled edge. Having placed orders for salads, both women now sat on the sun-flooded patio of a popular beachside restaurant. Geraniums filled a riot of clay pots. Soft classical music seemed in harmony with the ocean's natural rhythm. "My being there was an olive branch. Please know I never meant to hurt you."

Paisley nodded, refusing to acknowledge the knot blocking her throat.

"Prison was hard. As it should be. I learned a lot."

"You look good. Apparently, you landed on your feet?"

"Don't be cruel." Her mother reached across the table for her daughter's hands.

Paisley removed her hands from the table, drying sweaty palms on the thighs of her black maternity slacks.

"You're angry. I get that. When you were in college, and should have been coming home for long weekends and to do laundry, I was on lockdown. What I don't fully understand is why you're still so upset. Whatever you feel I did to you, I would like nothing more than to make amends. But to do that, I have to know what for."

Paisley took a fortifying sip of ice water before leaning in with her forearms pressed to the table. Keeping her voice low, she asked, "How can you be this oblivious and live with yourself? Because of you, I don't even know what a normal, healthy relationship looks like. I just threw away a wonderful man mostly because I don't feel worthy. I'm terrified the same wanderlust gene that kept you moving us every six months might be inside me. I might be a user like you. The love I think I feel for this man might really be more about a convenience factor you taught me all too well. I'm afraid I'm incapable of truly loving him, so instead, I'm using him."

"I'm sorry." Silent tears streamed down her mother's still beautiful cheeks. "I had you so young. I was only eighteen and when your father took off, and then died, I didn't know what to do. I had no career like you. No education. All I had were looks and a decent body I admittedly used to manipulate every man I could. I wanted to use them. Hurt them. I wanted them to feel as disposable as your father made me feel."

In the worst possible case of timing, their perky waitress delivered their meals and topped off their waters.

Like Wayne, Paisley left her so-called home at age eighteen. She'd had no friends in the many schools she'd attended, leaving her lots of time for study. Her good grades earned her scholarships that had funded her ultimate escape. College. Her first real friend had been Monica. A meaningful career and the satisfaction of owning a business rounded out her life, but it wasn't enough. Not nearly enough.

"The thing is," Paisley said to her mom, drawing a heart in her water glass's condensation, "you might have meant to make your many male targets feel disposable. But at the same time, your efforts had a similar effect on me."

"Oh, Paisley…" Her mom dabbed her perfectly made-up eyes with her napkin. "While I can never give you back all the years I wish I'd been a better mother, if you'd let me, I'd love nothing more than to start from scratch now." She withdrew a photo from her purse. It showed her arm in arm with a pleasant-looking man. They both wore leis. "This was taken on our honeymoon in Maui."

Typical.

Fresh out of prison, and already she'd found her latest mark.

"I can only imagine what you're thinking," her mom said. "Here I am again with another man, but this time it's different. We met at AA and he knows all my darkest secrets. He's an investment banker who also did time. It's a dark commonality, but out of pain we've forged new lives. I want that for you and your baby. The way Wayne looked at you was the kind of heartfelt meaning that up until meeting Gerald, I'd searched my whole life to find. You're so fortunate to have it now, while you're young. Grab hold of your man with both hands, and don't ever let go."

Not the least bit hungry, Paisley shoved her salad away.

"Congratulations. You always did seem to land on your feet. But here I am—"

"No." Her mother shook her head. "Right here and now, if there's nothing else you take from our meeting, I want you to stop playing the victim. Could your childhood and teen years been better? Absolutely. But that doesn't mean you get to use them as a crutch to avoid making big decisions for the rest of your life. I suspect you love Wayne every bit as much as he loves you, but you're too afraid to believe that love is real. Lasting. Because I taught you nothing that's good ever lasts, am I right?"

Silent tears streaming down her cheeks, Paisley nodded.

"All I ever wanted was for you to be my mom. What was wrong with me? Was I that unlovable?"

"Sweetheart…" She left her seat to wrap Paisley in a hug. "How can you not realize that for all those years you felt abandoned, I always felt as if you were my one bright constant? I love you so much. I just didn't know how to show that love. But I'm trying. Please try with me. Gerald and I live in La Jolla. I see a counselor every Wednesday. If you'd like, if I can find a time that works with your schedule. Would you please come?"

Paisley touched her tongue to the roof of her mouth to say no, but then saw the sincerity in her mother's hopeful smile. "*Please*. If you give me a chance, I'd like a do-over at being a mom to you and a grandmother to your son."

"Yes," Paisley whispered. But this time, she was the selfish one. On a soul-deep level, she finally realized that while Wayne might have been the one who more vocally resisted marriage, she was the one allowing old emotional scars to prevent new growth.

The only question now facing her was undoubtedly the most important—how would she get Wayne back into her life long enough for him to give her a second chance?

"ONE MORE PUSH, Paise." Monica held tight to one hand while Jules held her other.

"Your baby's crowning," said Dr. Stanley, her ob-gyn. "You can do it, Paisley. You're in the homestretch now."

"I'm so proud of you. You're almost there." With her free hand, Jules pressed a cool cloth to Paisley's forehead.

With all her might, Paisley bore down, *"Arggghhh!"*

The pain was beyond anything she'd ever imagined, but then came exquisite relief, along with the miraculous sound of her son's first bellowing cry.

Relief flooded her system, resulting in instant tears and laughter and unabashed joy. The only missing element in the scene was Wayne. But she planned on fixing that soon.

Her mother and Gerald were in the waiting room with Peter and Monica's parents. It was such an odd thing, planning the rest of her life around a man who had no idea he was included, but when a nurse placed tiny little John Wayne Jr. in Paisley's arms, she couldn't imagine spending the rest of her days with anyone but Wayne.

"He's gonna be a lady-killer." Monica gazed upon the infant with the serene smile of a woman anticipating her own baby's birth.

"I've never seen a more precious sight." Jules cupped her trembling hand to the crown of the baby's head. "You are going to be spoiled rotten, Baby Johnny."

"Jules," Paisley asked, "do you think Wayne will give me a second chance?"

"If he doesn't—" she tucked Paisley's hair behind her ears "—I'll ground him for life."

"I'm serious." Paisley held her son in the crook of her right arm, grasping Jules's hand with her left. "What should I do? I—I'm so sorry for the way we left things. There's so much to say."

"And you two will have your entire lifetimes to do exactly that. Now rest." She kissed Paisley's forehead. "Trust me, everything's going to work out fine."

Cradling her son, Paisley wished with all her heart she felt as confident about their shared future as Wayne's mom.

WAYNE DELIBERATELY TOOK his time gathering his gear and leaving the C-130 transport.

He dreaded seeing the happy families.

The dolled-up wives and girlfriends excited for a hot night with their men.

What did Wayne have? Squat.

He'd tried not being bitter about the way things turned out between Paisley and him, but it was kind of hard when he'd given her everything she'd professed to want, yet she'd still rejected him.

Normally, when a guy on the team got dumped, everyone gave him hell, but as if by an unspoken agreement, they'd all kept their pieholes shut. A fact for which he was profoundly grateful. How many guys could say they'd voluntarily had their hearts shredded not once, but twice?

He was one of the lucky few.

Veering across the tarmac, away from the crowd, Wayne took his Ray-Ban Aviators from a shirt pocket, slipped them on, then slapped his straw cowboy hat on top of his head.

The sun was too damned hot.

His mood was too damned foul.

He'd made it almost the three hundred yards to the hangar when he heard someone calling his name. He froze.

"Wayne! Wait up!"

He turned to find Paisley pushing a jogging stroller at a full-on run. Logan told him she'd had her baby. He didn't dare dwell on the news, since it would only make him more resentful of the fact that he hadn't been with her in the delivery room. Why was she here? Hadn't she already made it clear she wanted nothing more to do with him?

He should apologize for his harsh words, but he wasn't ready. Not yet. But soon.

"Hi…" She hunched over, badly out of breath.

"Hey." He fought the urge to reach out to her. At the very least, offering her a swig from his canteen.

"Monica told me your team was coming home today.

Hope you don't mind that she told a few fibs to get me on base."

"Let me get this straight." He lowered his sunglasses. "You refused to marry me because of lies, but you have no problem lying your way past armed guards onto a military base? You are some piece of work." He slid his sunglasses back in place—not to protect his eyes, but because he couldn't bear for her to know he was staring at the wonder of her baby boy. The boy he'd wanted to raise as his own. "Get to the point of why you're here, Paise. I need a beer and a shower."

Her eyes welled with tears while her lower lip quivered. "Don't you want to meet my baby?"

"I've seen him. He's cute."

"Guess his name."

"I couldn't care less." *Now, who's lying?* Turning his back on her so she couldn't see the pain no doubt as plain as the nose on his face, Wayne started walking again.

With her size mostly back to normal, she was faster than he'd grown used to. Even while steering the stroller, she caught up to drag him back around by his sleeve. "Ask my baby's name."

"What do you want from me? Why are you here?"

"I'm here to admit that back on the ranch, the night of our wedding, I was a fool. I'm sorry. So very sorry. If we live to a hundred, I'll spend the rest of our lives trying to make it up to you. Please, give me a second chance."

"Why?" *I want to give you as many chances as it takes to make you mine, but what's the point?* His heart felt in danger of pounding from his chest. "What changed that this time around anything would be different? Or that you'd keep your promise to never leave?"

"I talked to my mom. We're in counseling together. We still have a way to go, but things between us are better. I now see that it wasn't you I mistrusted, but myself. For years, I'd worked so hard not to be like her, that in some ways, I went in the opposite to the extreme. Instead of manipulating men to always provide, I've warred with myself to never need. But what I learned is that we all need. I especially need you. I love you. There, I said it, and I don't care who hears." She arched her head back and shouted, "I love Wayne Brustanovitch and want to be his wife!"

"Lord…" Unable to stop the grin tugging the corners of his lips, Wayne wasn't sure whether to laugh or cry or both. Was she for real? "You have changed."

"I told you." Gazing up at him expectantly, she asked, "Well? What do you think? Should we try again? This time from scratch—no fake engagement or fake cakes or anything fake. Only the real deal from here on out. What do you say?"

There was nothing to say.

A part of him was still scared this was all a dream. He'd wake back in Somalia with rockets screaming over his head.

"Wayne?" She'd taken the baby from his stroller, and now held him up for inspection. "Would you like to meet your namesake?"

"You can't be serious? You named him John Wayne Jr.?" She'd dressed the little guy in pint-size jeans, soft-sided cowboy boots and a T-shirt featuring a Trident and the slogan, My Daddy's a Navy SEAL.

She nodded. "Hope you don't mind me taking liberties with the shirt? Monica ordered one for their baby, so I had her get one for me, too. You know, just in case."

The emotion causing his eyes to tear and chest to swell was too much for one man to bear, so Wayne didn't even try. Instead, he pulled Paisley and their baby into his arms.

"I love you," he said into her hair. "I love our son. I love that we get to spend the next fifty or sixty years hashing out who really messed up our wedding."

"I'll take the hit," she said after gifting him with the kiss he only just realized he'd been waiting to return home to ever since leaving for deployment. "Although, you started the trouble by dunking me in the pool."

"I thought you enjoyed that?"

"I did, but I wouldn't be very smart if I let you know. I can't start a marriage having my guy believing he holds all the power."

Laughing, he removed his hat to settle it on the baby's head. Of course, it swallowed him whole. "He's gonna need a hat his own size. And a horse. I'll have to start looking right away for just the right one."

"Could he learn to walk before he rides?"

"Already sassing me, and we're not even married." He settled his free arm around her shoulders.

"Speaking of which, when you have leave, I promised your mom that if we got back together, we'd try again for another wedding at the ranch."

"Wait—my mom's been in on this, too?"

"And your dad. I love them both. Your mom and Monica helped me through the delivery. After all we put her through, I think it's only fair Jules gets her happy ending."

Wayne paused to kiss Paisley's nose, her cheeks and finally her lips. "I love you. Yes, to anything you want just as long as you never want to leave me again.

"As for you, big fella…" Taking the baby, he said, "We need to have a nice long talk about your future. What would you think about a career as a cowboy SEAL?"

Epilogue

"John Wayne Jr., don't throw hay at your baby sister."
Paisley's son may have only been a year old, but he was
already a pistol—walking early and wrapping his usually grubby and sticky hands on everything—including
the hay bales Peter, Wayne, Logan, Gerald and Paisley's
mom were setting out for the big Easter Sunday picnic
and egg hunt being held on the ranch.

"Cowboy, you come help Grandpoppa." Peter swept
Johnny up high, catching him midshriek in the air. With
the sun shining and not a breath of wind in the air, the
only sound came from a few fat bumblebees buzzing
on Jules's favorite pink sweetheart roses.

Even Bruce was enjoying the day by reclining in
his private pasture.

Paisley and Wayne's daughter was barely a month
old, big blue eyes open wide, taking in her world.

Not long after his return, Paisley and Wayne married in an intimate mountaintop ceremony with close
friends and family and a panoramic view of the world.

"I've never seen either of my men so happy," Jules
mused, sipping iced tea while comfy in her patio rocker.

"It has been an amazing year," Paisley said. "I feel incredibly blessed." And she was. She wasn't sure how, but every facet of her life had changed for the better. The forever family to which she'd always dreamed of belonging had become her new reality.

Never had she loved more or been loved more.

Construction had already started on the ranch's second hacienda—a wedding gift from Jules and Peter. Every chance they got, Paisley and Wayne left San Diego to help with construction or picking out finishes. By this time next year, Wayne would have retired from the Navy and be helping his father full-time with cattle breeding.

Paisley and Monica were opening a second design business in touristy Sedona.

"Whew." Monica rejoined them. She held Gigi in her arms. "That was a smelly diaper, ladybug."

Gigi grinned and giggled.

"How many people are you expecting tomorrow?" Paisley asked Jules.

"At least a couple hundred. Now that the babies are fed, we should get to work stuffing eggs with candy."

"Yes, ma'am." Monica jiggled her daughter. "Pretty soon you're going to be big enough to hunt for eggs, too. But until then, how about a nap?"

"Sounds good for you, too," Paisley said to her baby girl, Feathers, nicknamed for Angie Dickinson's character in *Rio Bravo*. Big surprise, the name had been her grandpoppa Peter's idea. Her given name was Julia Katherine, in honor of her paternal grandmother.

Wayne sauntered up from the field.

Would there ever come a day when the mere sight of him didn't give her heart a thrill? Even dressed in jeans, cowboy boots, a T-shirt and his trusty straw hat, the breadth of his shoulders and love behind his gaze never failed to stir her.

"Mom? Do you mind if I borrow my wife?"

"You can have her for about fifteen minutes, but then we're getting started on stuffing the eggs."

"Yes, ma'am." He took the baby from Paisley, holding her in the crook of his muscular arm before helping her momma from her chair.

"What's up?" Paisley asked out of earshot from the patio.

"I wanted to run something by you."

"Okay?"

He slipped his free arm around her, pulling her close enough for a leisurely kiss, but not to wake their now sleeping baby.

"Mmm…" Pausing for air, she asked, "I could talk about that all day. But what did you need?"

"You." He kissed her again.

"Are you trying to get me in trouble with your mom?"

He laughed. "Maybe I've developed a thing for bad girls?"

"You're crazy."

"About you." He kissed her thoroughly. "I don't tell you enough—I love you." He smiled at her so sweetly. "What would you think about having another baby?"

Paisley coughed. "Two babies in two years are plenty. But thanks for asking."

"I'm messing with you. I love our family just the way it is."

"Me, too."

"But I would be amenable to a puppy."

"A small puppy?"

"Aren't they all?"

"I mean a small breed. No Great Danes or shepherds."

"You're not thinking like a toy breed, are you? I can't see myself with a Yorkie or Chihuahua."

Several months later, on Christmas day at the ranch, beneath the tree holding twinkling white lights and their pair of fake cake cowboy ornaments, Paisley, Jules and Peter clapped and laughed as Wayne opened his last gift of the morning—a one-pound Yorkshire terrier puppy named Duke.

* * * * *

Don't miss the previous books in
Laura Marie Altom's COWBOY SEALS *series:*

THE BABY AND THE COWBOY SEAL
THE SEAL'S SECOND CHANCE BABY
THE COWBOY SEAL'S JINGLE BELL BABY
THE COWBOY SEAL'S CHRISTMAS BABY

Available now from Harlequin Western Romance!

We hope you enjoyed this story from
Harlequin® Western Romance.

Harlequin® Western Romance is coming to an
end, but community, cowboys and true love are
here to stay. Starting July 2018, discover more
heartfelt tales of family and friendship from
Harlequin® Special Edition.

Romance is for life, and these stories show that
every chapter in a relationship has its challenges
and delights and that love can be
renewed with each turn of the page!

Look for six *new* romances every month
from **Harlequin® Special Edition!**
Available wherever books are sold.

Get 2 Free Books,

Plus 2 Free Gifts—

just for trying the Reader Service!

Eyes widening, she gasped. "Ryder."

"Hello, Becca."

"Hi." Her gaze darted briefly to the small boy next to
her. "This is a surprise."

"That's an understatement." Ryder did a quick mental
calculation. The boy would've been two years old when
Becca's grandmother died. As far as he knew, Shirley
hadn't mentioned anything about Becca having a kid.
And when it came to what little news they got about
Amy and Becca in LA, his mom never skipped a word.

"Right." She cleared her throat. "I planned on calling
you and your mom later."

He raised his eyebrows.

"You know, after we settled in. We just got to town
an hour ago."

Okay, maybe she was telling the truth. But why look
so nervous? "I hope by *we* you mean Amy," he said,
holding Becca's gaze. "Is she here?"

She shook her head. Sadness flickered in her hazel eyes before she blinked and looked away. "I think she had other plans for the—" She pressed her lips together and swallowed.

"What? For Thanksgiving? Let's see, that makes seven of them that she's missed now?"

"I'm not her keeper," Becca said, her voice barely a whisper. "Your sister does what she wants."

"Aunt Amy gave me a neato truck." The kid grinned up at him. "You wanna see it?"

Ryder felt a surge of relief. He didn't know what had given him the sick feeling that something bad had happened to Amy. If that were true, she wouldn't be buying the kid toys. "Hey, sport."

"Sport?" The boy wrinkled his nose. "My name is Noah."

"Sorry, Noah. I'm Ryder." He stuck his hand out. The kid slapped his palm against Ryder's and started giggling.

In spite of himself, Ryder smiled. Whatever was up with Amy wasn't Becca's son's fault. Ryder was seven years older than his sister and hadn't paid much attention to her friends, but he remembered Becca.

When he looked back up at her, he saw the tears in her eyes before she blinked them away.

The relief he'd felt moments ago disappeared. Something was wrong, and Becca knew the truth.

Don't miss TO TRUST A RANCHER by Debbi Rawlins, available May 2018 wherever Harlequin® Western Romance books and ebooks are sold.

www.Harlequin.com

HWREXP0418

Looking for more satisfying love stories
with community and family at their core?

Check out **Harlequin® Special Edition**
and **Harlequin® Western Romance** books!

New books available every month!

HFGENRE2017R

Need an adrenaline rush from nail-biting tales
(and irresistible males)?

Check out **Harlequin® Intrigue®**
and **Harlequin® Romantic Suspense** books!

New books available every month!

CONNECT WITH US AT:

Harlequin.com/Community

 Facebook.com/HarlequinBooks

 Twitter.com/HarlequinBooks

 Instagram.com/HarlequinBooks

 Pinterest.com/HarlequinBooks

ReaderService.com

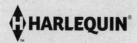

**ROMANCE WHEN
YOU NEED IT**